"Put me down!"

She fought him the best she could, a hundred and twenty pounds of wriggling fury. "Don't do this. Whatever you think you are doing, I know you are going to regret it."

He did already.

"Are you crazy?"

He could get them out of there, away from the grenade blast site, in a hurry. He fitted his free hand to her shapely behind to hold her place. Smooth skin, lean limbs, *dangerous* curves. He tried not to touch more than was absolutely necessary. Yeah, she could probably make him do a couple of crazy things without half trying.

And if they made it out alive he'd be tempted to find out what those were.

DANA MARTON

TALL, DARK
AND
LETHAL

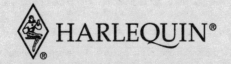

TORONTO • NEW YORK • LONDON
AMSTERDAM • PARIS • SYDNEY • HAMBURG
STOCKHOLM • ATHENS • TOKYO • MILAN • MADRID
PRAGUE • WARSAW • BUDAPEST • AUCKLAND

With many thanks to Allison Lyons, Louise Rozett and Priya Ravishankar for all their help, and to my family for their never-ending support.

Recycling programs
for this product may
not exist in your area.

ISBN-13: 978-0-373-69372-6
ISBN-10:   0-373-69372-9

TALL, DARK AND LETHAL

www.eHarlequin.com

Printed in U.S.A.

ABOUT THE AUTHOR

Dana Marton is the author of over a dozen fast-paced, action-adventure romantic suspense novels and a winner of the Daphne du Maurier Award of Excellence. She loves writing books of international intrigue, filled with dangerous plots that try her tough-as-nails heroes and the special women they fall in love with. Her books have been published in seven languages in eleven countries around the world. When not writing or reading, she loves to browse antique shops and enjoys working in her sizable flower garden where she searches for "bad" bugs with the skills of a superspy and vanquishes them with the agility of a commando soldier. Every day in her garden is a thriller. To find more information on her books, please visit www.danamarton.com. She would love to hear from her readers and can be reached via e-mail at the following address: DanaMarton@DanaMarton.com.

Books by Dana Marton

HARLEQUIN INTRIGUE

CAST OF CHARACTERS

Bailey Preston—When her home is destroyed by terrorists, her only hope is her mysterious neighbor, Cade Palmer. But can she trust him, or is he the source of her troubles?

Cade Palmer—He retired from the SDDU, but his enemies seem to be reluctant to let him go. And then there is the one man he had sworn to kill or die trying. Except that he keeps getting distracted by the beauty next door.

Zak Preston—Is he just a troubled teen, or has he crossed the line?

David Smith—Once an informant, he has chosen the dark side and is responsible for the death of dozens. He is hiding in Indonesia. Or is he?

Colonel Wilson—Head of the Special Designation Defense Unit.

SDDU—Special Designation Defense Unit, a top secret military team established to fight terrorism. Its existence is known by only a select few. Members are recruited from the best of the best.

Chapter One

He would kill a man before the day was out. And—
God help him—Cade Palmer hoped this would be
the last time.

He'd done the job before and didn't like the
strange heaviness that settled on him. Not guilt or
second thoughts—he'd been a soldier too long for
that. But still, something grim and somber that made
little sense, especially today. He'd been waiting for
this moment for months. Today he would put an old
nightmare to rest and fulfill a promise.

In an hour, Abhi would hand him information on
David Smith's whereabouts, and there was no place
on earth he couldn't reach by the end of the day. He'd
hire a private jet if he had to. Whatever it took. *Before
the sun comes up tomorrow, David Smith will be gone.*

He headed up the stairs to his cell phone as it rang
on his nightstand. Wiping the last of the gun oil on his
worn jeans, he crossed into his bedroom. He was about
to reach for the phone when he caught sight of the
unmarked van parked across the road from his house.

The van hadn't been there thirty minutes ago. Nor had he seen it before. He made it his business to pay attention to things like that. At six in the morning on Saturday, his new suburban Pennsylvania neighborhood was still asleep, the small, uniform yards deserted. Nothing was out of place—except the van, which made the hair on the back of his neck stand up.

The only handgun he kept inside the house—a SIG P228—was downstairs on the kitchen table in pieces, half-cleaned. He swore. Trouble had found him once again—par for the course in his line of work. Just because he was willing to let go of his old enemies—except David Smith—didn't mean they were willing to let go of him.

"Happy blasted retirement," he said under his breath as he turned to get the rifle he kept in the hallway closet. From the corner of his eye, he caught movement. The rear door of the van inched open, and with a sick sense of dread, he knew what he was going to see a split second before the man in the back was revealed, lifting a grenade launcher to his shoulder.

Instinct and experience. Cade had plenty of both and put them to good use, shoving the still-ringing phone into his back pocket as he lunged for the hallway.

Had he been alone in the house, his plan would have been simple: get out and make those bastards rue the day they were born. But he wasn't alone, which meant he had to alter his battle plan to include grabbing the most obnoxious woman in the universe—aka his neighbor, who lived in the other half of his duplex—and dragging her from the kill zone.

He darted through his bare guest bedroom and busted open the door that led to the small balcony in the back, crashing out into the muggy August morning. Heat, humidity and birdsong.

At least the birds in the jungle knew when danger was afoot. These twittered on, clueless. Proximity to civilization dulled their instincts. And his. He should have known that trouble was coming before it got here. Should have removed himself to some cabin in the woods, someplace with a warning system set up and an arsenal at his fingertips, a battleground where civilians wouldn't have been endangered. But he was where he was, so he turned his thoughts to escape and evasion as he moved forward.

Bailey Preston's half of the house was the mirror image of his, except that she used the back room for her bedroom. Cade vaulted over her balcony, kicked her new French door open and zeroed in on the tufts of cinnamon hair sticking out from under a pink, flowered sheet on a bed that took up most of her hot-pink bedroom. Beneath the mess of hair, a pair of blue-violet eyes were struggling to come into focus. She blinked at him like a hungover turtle. Her mouth fell open but no sound came out. Definitely a first.

He strode forward without pause.

"What are you doing here? Get away from me!" She'd woken up in that split second it took him to reach her bed and was fairly shrieking. She was good at that—she'd been a thorn in his side since he'd moved in. She was pulling the sheet to her chin, scampering away from him, flailing in the tangled covers. "Don't you touch me. You, you—"

He unwrapped her with one smooth move and picked her up, ignoring the pale-purple silk shorts and tank top. So Miss Clang-and-Bang had a soft side. Who knew?

"Don't get your hopes up. I'm just getting you out."

She weighed next to nothing but still managed to be an armful. Smelled like sleep and sawdust, with a faint hint of varnish thrown in. Her odd scent appealed to him more than any coy, flowery perfume could have. Not that he was in any position to enjoy it. He tried in vain to duck the small fists pounding his shoulders and head, and gave thanks to God that her nephew, who'd been vacationing with her for the first part of summer, had gone back to wherever he'd come from. Dealing with her was all he could handle.

"Are you completely crazy?" She was actually trying to poke his eyes out. "I'm calling the police. I'm calling the police right now!"

She was possibly more than he could handle, although that macho sense of vanity that lived deep down in every man made it hard for him to admit that, even as her fingers jabbed dangerously close to his irises in some freakish self-defense move she must have seen on TV.

"You might want to hang on." He was already out of the room. Less than ten seconds had passed since he'd seen the guy in the van. "And try to be quiet." He stepped up to the creaking balcony railing and jumped before it could give way under their combined weight.

She screamed all the way down and then some, giving no consideration to his eardrums whatsoever. Once upon a time, he'd worked with explosives on a regular basis. He knew loud. She was it.

He swore at the pain that shot up his legs as they crashed to the ground, but he was already pushing away with her over his shoulder and running for cover in the maze of Willow Glen duplexes in Chadds Ford, Pennsylvania.

Unarmed. In the middle of freaking combat.

He didn't feel fear—just unease. He was better than this. He'd always had a sixth sense that let him know when his enemies were closing in. It wasn't like him to get lulled into complacency.

"Are you trying to kill us? Are you on drugs? Listen. To. Me. Try to focus." She grabbed his chin and turned his face to hers. "I am your neighbor."

He kept the house between him and the tangos in the van, checking for any indication of danger waiting for them ahead. No movement on the rooftops. If there was a sniper, he was lying low. Cade scanned the grass for wire trips first, then for anything he could use as a makeshift weapon. He came up with nada.

"Put me down!" She fought him as best she could, a hundred and twenty pounds of wriggling fury. "Don't do this! Whatever you think you are doing, I know you are going to regret it."

He did already.

"Are you crazy?"

He could get there in a hurry. He put his free hand

on her shapely behind to hold her in place. Smooth skin, lean limbs, dangerous curves. He tried not to grope more than was absolutely necessary. Yeah, she could probably make him do a couple of crazy things without half trying. But they had to get out of the kill zone first.

"Let me go! Listen, let me—"

They were only a dozen or so feet from the nearest duplex when his home—and hers—finally blew.

That shut her up.

He dove forward, into the cover of the neighbor's garden shed. They went down hard, and he rolled on top of her, protecting her from the blast, careful to keep most of his weight off. The second explosion came right on the heels of the first. It shook the whole neighborhood.

That would be the C4 he kept in the safe in his garage.

Damn.

"What—was—that?" Her blue-violet eyes stared up at him, her voice trembling, her face the color of lemon sherbet.

There were days when she looked like a garden fairy in her flyaway, flower-patterned clothes with a mess of cinnamon hair, petite but well-rounded body, big violet eyes and the cutest pixie nose he'd ever seen on a woman. She had no business being wrapped in silk in his arms, looking like a frightened sex kitten as he lay on top of her.

Her fear quickly turned to rage, unfortunately.

"What did you do?" Her tone was a good reminder

that even when she did look like a fairy, she wasn't the "flit from flower to flower" kind found in children's books. She was more like the angry fairies in Irish folktales, the kind that throw thunderbolts from their eyes and put wicked curses on men.

Just like her to blame him for the slightest thing that went wrong around the house. She had blamed him for the molehills the week before. Supposedly, he'd used the kind of lawn fertilizer that attracted the little bastards.

"You blew up the house?" Her full mouth really did lose all attractiveness when it went tight with anger. A shame.

Okay, so he did have a small collection of explosives left over from previous missions. Not that he was going to mention the C4 to her just now. Or ever. She was about the least understanding person he knew, with a tendency to harp on people's mistakes. His, anyway.

And he hadn't made any mistakes here, dammit. The C4 had been secured. He was retired at a secret location—or so he thought. The last thing he'd expected was a grenade blasting through his house.

"I didn't blow up anything. We need to get out of here." Before everyone in the whole development rushed outside, and the cops arrived.

"I have to ask the neighbors to call the police." She was scampering away in a tempting display of bare limbs.

Her skin was smooth and soft but barely tanned, even at the end of summer. When she wasn't at work at the garden center, she was hammering around in her garage. Not the type to lie out on her balcony in a skimpy bikini like their neighbor across the street, and Cade gave thanks for that. There was only so much temptation a man could take.

"I'm sure that's taken care of already." He grabbed her slim arm, registering the velvet feel of her skin as he pulled her up. A wave of smoke and dust reached them. "Keep your mouth and your nose covered."

The top of her head came only to his chin. Not that anyone would think of her as a fragile little thing. Her feistiness had always lent her stature. But that feistiness was nowhere to be seen now as she stared, coughing, toward what had been her home. Wood beams leaned on each other like some macabre game of pick-up sticks, furniture strewn and burning all over the lawn. She looked lost, blinking more rapidly with each passing second.

Bailey Preston lost. That'd be the day. The smoke and dust must be distorting his vision.

"Keep low. Keep in cover." He moved out, pulling her behind him, covering ground at a good clip. He needed to get her as far away as possible before the shock wore off and she started fighting him tooth and nail again.

He headed straight for the grove of trees that separated their development from the next, taking advantage of the burning house that captured the full attention of the people who were coming outside in robes and pajamas, looking stunned. Bailey blended right in with her silk pajamas. Which didn't mean she wasn't attention worthy. He was still trying hard not to look.

"We have to go back." She did her best to stop him.

He kept going, pulling her completely into the trees. In thirty seconds, they were in a more upscale neighborhood, with mansions on a full acre each, lush green lawns and professionally done flower beds, a few of which showed off Bailey's handmade garden-art pieces. He went around an oversize pool and up a few steps to a driveway, heading for the nearest car—a Cadillac Escalade.

Nobody stirred in the house. The power couple was probably golfing at the crack of dawn in their vintage Corvette that he had admired from afar. He had thoroughly checked out his new neighborhood and its surroundings before he had moved in, planning escape routes. Except he hadn't planned on taking someone with him when and if he had to run. That changed things a little. Instead of going for his secret stash of weapons and circling back to see who had found him, he decided to keep Bailey Preston safe and book the hell out of here before anyone came after them.

The Escalade was unlocked. After two months of living out here, he still couldn't believe people did that.

"What are you doing?" She was beginning to fight in earnest again, but he easily kept his hold on her slim wrist. "The police will want to talk to us."

Just the thing they needed to avoid. "Get in." He pushed her into the car and slid across the hood, bursting inside and catching her, pulling her back just as she was about to light out. He clicked on the child-proof locks. "Hang on for a second."

No keys above the visor. Even trusting suburbanites had their limits. A damn shame. Not that hot-wiring the thing took all that long. They were pulling out of the driveway in less than a minute.

"Get down."

"Where are we going?" Her voice still held tinges of shock and confusion, but her blue-violet eyes cleared as her gaze pinned him. "Why are you stealing a car?"

He kind of liked her dazed and confused—definitely easier to handle. Not that easy played a big part in his life. "Look, we need to go someplace safe."

"*I* need to get back to my house." Her voice now rang with resolution as she reached for the door again, grunting in frustration when it wouldn't open. "What are you doing? You have to let me go."

Clearly, she didn't have a very good grasp on the situation. "The people who blew up the house are still out there." He spelled it out for her. To be fair, this was likely the first time she had been shot at with a grenade launcher. He should cut her some slack.

"Gas explosion," she said, with full conviction.

He wished. Wouldn't that make his life so much simpler? "I don't think so." He scanned the street as he drove, looking for the van or any other vehicles or activity. He couldn't be sure how many men were out there after him. Anyone he'd tangled with in the past would know him enough to come prepared.

"Nobody is trying to kill us, for crying out loud.

What are you? An army veteran? What do they call it?" She furrowed her delicate brows. "Combat fatigue? Is that why you're so paranoid?"

Combat fatigue? She was going to put him on the disabled roster? He didn't think so.

"Maybe I think someone blew up the damn house on purpose because I saw the bastard aiming his grenade launcher. How is that?" Impatience showed in his words, but he didn't care. He was supposed to be heading off to an important meeting with Abhi, dammit. A meeting he had put off for too long.

Or not long enough.

Had getting in touch with some of his old connections in the field triggered this attack? The timing was a little too close for comfort.

She was staring at him wide-eyed and speechless. Stayed that way for another full second. Had to be a record. "You— What? Who?"

"Damned if I know." He glanced in the rearview mirror. "But we are not going back there until I figure out what's going on."

A few seconds of silence passed while she mulled that over. He expected her to issue another passionate argument for returning. But when she finally spoke, all she said was, "I don't have clothes on." And she crossed her arms in front of her.

Soft, silky skin and barely concealed curves. *Just keep looking at the road.*

"I noticed that." Yes, sir. Certainly had. He cleared his throat before he chanced another glance at her.

Pink washed over her cheeks.

Wasn't she just a surprise and a half? Looked like having her house blown up brought her defenses down.

His house, too. The full implications fully registered. His hideout. The one place he'd felt sure he would be safe. Where he'd planned on starting over.

Apparently not. A four-letter word slipped from his mouth with some vehemence.

She glared at him, but sirens sounding in the distance claimed her attention. "Who wants you dead?" she asked after a minute.

He considered the endless list in his head as he pulled out of the maze of developments and onto Route 1. The last batch of terrorists he'd tangled with had certainly promised to hunt him down and kill him like a dog. But they were only the latest addition to a large group. His occupation was what you'd call "conflict heavy."

"Then again, the *who doesn't* list is probably shorter," she said, without waiting for his answer.

He bit back a grin. Her griping got on his nerves more often than not, but there was a sassy side to her that he found entertaining. Half the time he wanted her to win a trip to the moon. What he wanted the other half of the time was what kept him up at night.

Her bedroom was now fixed in his brain. *Pink silk sheets.* He could have lived without knowing that. Fortunately, he didn't have much time to ponder it.

He considered the events of the morning. How much of what he knew and who he was should he share with her? As little as possible. He didn't think she'd feel better if he told her that the tangos didn't want him dead—yet. Otherwise they would have hit his bedroom and not the garage.

Two single garages sat side by side in the front of the duplex, right in the middle. From the speed with which the second explosion followed the first, it was clear to Cade that the hit went straight to the garage and then ignited the C4. Losing that hurt more than losing the house. Not that he thought the tangos knew he had an explosive stash. They just wanted to hit something other than the bedroom and give Cade time to rush outside so they could pick him up in the confusion.

But he'd seen them in time and made it out. And then, before they could come after him, they had been rocked by the second explosion. Their van was close to the house—just across the road. If Bailey weren't with him, he could have gone back to check it out. Could be it had sustained damage and was still stuck there.

Could be they had a backup plan and he would be walking straight into it.

He pulled the phone from his pocket and checked his missed call. The Colonel, head of the Special Designation Defense Unit. Just the man he needed to talk to. He hit the dial button.

"Sir, I have a small problem. I need to come in," he said as soon as the Colonel picked up. "I'm not alone." He could have dropped Miss Scream-and-Holler off at her nearest friend's house, but she needed to be read the riot act about the confidentiality of what had gone down this morning. As far as her neighbors would be concerned, the explosion *had* been a damn gas leak.

Someone would take care of Bailey to ensure that she was fully aware of the gravity of the situation as well as run a background check on her before they released her. Not that they would find much of interest. He had run a check himself before he had moved into their duplex.

He would go underground for a while. The SDDU, from which he had recently retired, had safe rooms available on various army bases around the country, as well as safe houses in the civilian world. He'd be directed to one where he could recoup and rearm so he could start figuring out what was going on.

"I've been trying to reach you," the Colonel said, his tone grimmer than hell in a heat wave. And he hadn't even heard all the bad news for the morning yet.

"Somebody just blew up my house." Straight to the point always worked best with the Colonel. "Any chance of getting a list of everyone I've done business with who has entered the country in the past six months?"

He could hear the man draw a slow breath. "You bet. Not that I can think of any off the top of my head."

That didn't bode well. The Colonel kept a close eye on the comings and goings of anyone on their tagged list.

"Could be they came through the southern border without us knowing, or through one of the ports," Cade said, thinking out loud.

"It's a possibility," he acknowledged. A moment of silence passed. "A month out of the action and you're looking for trouble already? I thought you said you were going for the quiet life."

Cade shifted in his seat. "I was, sir. But it looks like the past isn't finished with me yet." The Colonel didn't need to know that he'd been staging his very last—private—op for weeks. He didn't want to drag anyone into that with him.

"How could anyone find you? *I* don't even know where you are."

An exaggeration. The Colonel knew everything. Or could find out in a hurry. "No idea yet, sir, but I'll figure it out."

When his cover had been blown in Southeast Asia a little over four months ago, and his life further complicated by shrapnel in his lungs, he'd been retired from undercover commando work at the age of forty. A retirement his enemies seemed unwilling to honor. He couldn't blame them. He'd done some damage in his day.

But he hadn't thought he would be found, not this fast. He had counted on having enough time to take care of his unfinished business with that bastard Smith before he would have to disappear again.

He hadn't even known about the uncle who had left him half of a duplex in Pennsylvania. His grandmother had had an older son out of wedlock that she had never told her husband and daughter about. A son who, apparently, had died not long ago with no children of his own, so Cade ended up with the house.

And he'd received his payoff from the SDDU in cash. He hadn't been to a bank since he'd been shipped back stateside from the military hospital in Germany. Hadn't used credit cards, hadn't returned to his old home or any of his properties to retrieve as much as a coffee cup, hadn't gotten his car out of storage. He might as well have died on that last mission and never returned to the U.S. No one knew where he was.

Except the tangos who had just blown up his house.

"Where can I go, sir? What's open?" The sooner he got off the road, the sooner he could start investigating, the sooner he could take care of the men in the van and get back to the op he'd been planning. Which would now be delayed, dammit. Didn't look like he would be catching up with Smith today after all.

Bailey pulled her legs up to hug her knees. She needed to put some decent clothes on. He tried not to look at her toned legs. She was barefoot, her toenails done in pink.

He wasn't sure he could take any more pink this morning. Fortunately, she quickly released her knees and set her feet down.

"Do not come in." The Colonel enunciated each word.

That snapped him back to business. "Sir?"

"The FBI is looking for you. There was an Agent Rubliczky here at the crack of dawn. He's not happy. That's why I called earlier."

"What do they want now?" He had left the FBI for the SDDU under less than amicable circumstances that included an inside, undercover job to find a leak. His work had ruffled a lot of feathers at the Bureau. He knew Rubliczky by reputation. The man worked domestic terrorism. His blood ran cold at the implications. *Son of a bitch.*

"I'm being set up?" It seemed impossible for someone there to carry a grudge this long. He'd left the Bureau nearly a decade ago.

"They think you're involved in something. It's pretty bad, Cade. They are out for blood. They are also talking about a Bailey Preston. Who is she to you?"

A distraction the magnitude of which could barely be expressed. "We shared the same duplex. She has nothing to do with this." He stole a glance at her from the corner of his eye and couldn't help noticing her nipples nearly pushing through the thin silk top. He liked to think he was a pretty disciplined guy, but still, he was only a man.

"You're sure? She could be into…whatever. Could even be a foreign asset."

Against his better judgment, he looked at Bailey full on. He'd been in this business long enough to be a fair judge of character. "Not possible."

"She is on their list, too. Could be dangerous."

He watched as she twisted an arm around, looking straight ahead and trying to keep him from noticing that she was working on pulling up the door lock, yanking it hard enough to nearly break it off. Her jerky movements were giving her full breasts a soft bounce. And he knew exactly what they would feel like moving against his palms.

"It would be better if you stayed put for a while until I figure out what's going on," the Colonel was saying.

Stay put where? All he had was the Escalade, which could be reported stolen any minute. He couldn't go back to the duplex—or to any of his other properties. He couldn't go to the law, and he couldn't stay on the road. There were some badass terrorists looking for him, along with the FBI. And if that wasn't crazy enough, he had his ill-tempered neighbor in the silk pajamas to worry about.

He'd run for his life many times before, but never with a half-naked woman in tow. Most guys he knew would say the addition of a half-naked woman would improve just about any situation a man could get into.

She flashed him a look sharp enough to peel skin, her blue-violet eyes throwing thunderbolts once again. Her normally generous lips tightened to a thin line as she forced her words through them. "I'm going to sue you for this."

Those guys had never met Bailey Preston, that's for sure.

Chapter Two

"Take me home or take me to the nearest police station. Your pick," Bailey said for the umpteenth time, raising her voice a smidgen, which made no difference whatsoever. Talking to Cade Palmer was like talking to her garden statuettes, or to her sixteen-year-old nephew, Zak, who was going through yet another difficult phase. Poor kid.

She was willing to cut Zak some slack. But not Cade. Cade was a grown man who should be held responsible for his actions.

"Who are you, anyway?" Even sitting down, she had to look up at him. He was a head taller, built but lean, and irritating as anything.

She was starting to suspect that he wasn't the computer programmer he'd claimed to be. People didn't come after computer programmers with grenade launchers. Then there was all that "yes, sir; no, sir" business on the phone, and him wanting to "come in."

He was looking in the rearview mirror and ignoring her. Straight nose, strong jawline and short-cropped dark brown hair. He had a singular focus and an easy grace to his lean body.

"Are you in the witness protection program?"

He took forever to respond. "Kind of."

Oh, God. Anger flooded her circuits. He had no right to drag her into his dirty business. "Could you be any vaguer?"

"You bet." He looked at her with his caramel brown eyes, which were fringed with thick, dark lashes. "There's a confidentiality issue."

What on earth had she ever done to deserve this from the universe?

She had to be honest—she didn't much care for the man. He was insufferable for the most part, the kind of neighbor people prayed wouldn't move in next door. She did her best not to let him get a rise out of her with every outrageous act or comment—and failed often. And she had trained herself not to ogle or respond to his magnificent body, not even if he purposely taunted her by mowing the lawn in nothing but a pair of tattered blue jeans. But his eyes got to her every time. And there was no avoiding them, because if she dropped her gaze, she was confronted with his mile-wide chest.

"It's for your own protection," he added.

"I don't want your kind of protection." She was lucky he hadn't killed her when they'd jumped from the balcony. Her heart raced all over again just thinking about it. Or maybe she just hadn't had a chance to calm down fully yet.

He had stepped up on her railing—which she

should have replaced when she'd installed the French doors, but had run out of money—and then he had stepped out into nothing. *Air.* His arms had been like steel brackets around her. For a surreal moment, he had morphed into some kind of action hero. Or villain. She hadn't quite decided yet which one.

"I don't want to go with you."

"Too bad," he said, without looking at her.

That was *so* like the man. Stubborn and rude. Insufferable. From the moment he had moved in, they had fought over everything, from the noise she made working in her garage to the oil his car leaked all over the driveway. He'd claimed her music was too loud. He'd knocked over her favorite flagpole and flat out refused to fix it. He might have a great body and gorgeous eyes, but manners he had none.

He'd had the gall to yell at Zak for tapping into his wireless. Why? It didn't cost him any extra if Zak used it. She had dial-up, but Zak had wanted something faster. The troubled teen—who, by the way, was a computer genius, but would Cade notice that and take him under his wing a little? Oh, noooo— did deserve some distraction when his life as he knew it was falling apart. Cade Palmer was selfish and mean to kids.

And a kidnapper.

"You can't take me God knows where against my will. Explain to me why we can't go to the police."

"This is beyond the police. As soon as I can be sure that it's safe to let you go, I will. Put on your seat belt."

So she couldn't easily jump from the car when he stopped for a light? Not a chance. "What do you mean, beyond the police?"

He ignored her, which made her want to beat him over the head with something. Just her luck that he'd stolen a car without as much as a baseball bat on the backseat. "Where are we going?"

He took a sharp turn, and she slid hard into the door. She shot him a glare before reaching for her seat belt.

"Stay low." He picked up speed, then took two turns in quick succession, watching the rearview mirror more closely than the road ahead of them.

Oh. Her mouth went dry as she gripped her seat. All she could think of was the way he had said "grenade launcher" with that dark look on his face just a short while ago. Her heart skipped a beat. "Are they following us?"

Long moments passed before he responded, slowing the car at last. "We're fine. For a second I thought—"

"You gave me a heart attack for nothing?" She went for the door lock again. When he reached over and grabbed her hand, she shoved hard against him. Not that he took any notice. "Want to tell me where you're taking me?"

"We need a new car and some weapons." He pulled up to the post office and parked.

How did they get here? Clearly, he knew more back roads than she did. Maybe he wasn't as new to the neighborhood as he'd claimed. Although she'd never seen him before he'd shown up three months ago just to annoy her to death.

"Come on. We're going in."

"In pajamas? Barefoot?" Her mind suddenly caught up with what he'd said. "Weapons?" Her voice was a touch weaker on that last word.

"It's not even seven in the morning. Nobody is going to be in there. You're fine."

Obviously he wasn't the kind of man who worried much about propriety. But he was right; the building was empty. The post office wasn't open yet, but the room with the P.O. boxes was. He went straight to the stainless-steel sorting table that housed forms of all sizes and colors, reached under it, searched for a second and then came up with a small key. He opened one of the larger, business-size P.O. boxes on the opposite wall and retrieved a box that held a black gym bag.

Once they returned to the car, he tossed the bag in the back and indicated that she should get in. "You should be able to find something in there to wear. You can change here."

Huh?

Getting naked with Cade Palmer nearby wasn't on her it-might-happen-in-this-lifetime list. Although there had been that dream…. Okay, maybe more than one. But she was not going to think about them—not now, not ever. She opened the bag and saw a soft, extra-large T-shirt on top. She would be less conspicuous in that than in her slinky pajama top.

"Fine. Don't look." She turned her back to him.

He started the car and pulled out of the parking lot. "I try not to make promises I can't keep."

She could tell from his voice that he was grinning. Insufferable.

She grabbed the bottom of her top. Stalled. Looked back at him. He lifted his gaze to the rearview mirror.

"Don't look!"

"You turned around. I thought you wanted something from me." He turned his attention back to the road. She was right—he *was* grinning.

She yanked her silk top off. No big deal. He had probably seen a naked woman or two before, anyway. It would have been easier to leave the top on under the T-shirt, but it was the middle of a heat wave, the temperature nearing ninety already—not a day for layers.

She glanced down at her body. With his long T-shirt on top, the silk shorts almost passed for street wear. She dug into the bag, hoping for something for her feet. Her soles were scratched and bruised from him dragging her—barefoot—through all that landscaping.

Flip-flops would have been great. Instead, she found a Ziploc bag full of IDs and bank cards, and a wad of cash held together by a rubber band.

And a gun.

Her fingertips went cold, the air suddenly froze in her lungs, and clothing became the least of her problems. His mentioning weapons was one thing; sitting next to a nasty-looking firearm was another. It brought the severity of her situation into sharp focus.

"I'll take that." He held his hand out and, when after a moment of hesitation, she gingerly gave him the gun, he said, "See if you can find some bullets in the front pocket."

She did. A whole box of them. She handed them over, and he started to load the handgun without slowing down or taking his eyes off the road, driving with one elbow. Like he was one of those guys in spy movies who practice taking apart and putting together their weapons while blindfolded. If she weren't so scared, she would have been impressed.

She considered staying in the backseat, as far from him as possible. But she had questions, and she wanted to look at his face while he answered them to see if he was lying to her.

She climbed to the front, nearly knocking him out with her left knee when she slipped—which she didn't feel too bad about, to be honest—then fastened herself in. First things first. "Why is the Mafia after you?" She braced herself for some grizzly story. It had to be something pretty serious.

He gave her a blank look.

"Witness protection?" she prompted.

The tanned skin around his caramel eyes crinkled. "I never said anything about the Mafia."

She thought back. True. She'd assumed.

"You did witness a crime, right? That's how people get into witness protection." What did she know about that, anyway? Whatever she'd seen on TV. And real cops always said how those shows were wildly inaccurate.

Still, if he was in the program, there had to be a good reason for it. She hoped he wasn't a criminal who'd rolled over on his buddies. She pulled as far away from him as possible without being too obvious about it, and put on the best poker face she could, preparing for his answer.

"I'm not in witness protection."

She glared. "You said—"

"I said *kind of.*"

She really should have asked more questions *before* she handed him the gun. Oh, God. She'd just armed the man who had kidnapped her. Stupid, stupid, stupid. She was so far out of her element, she couldn't keep up, couldn't think fast enough. She had to start using her head to gain some information and make some decisions. "Any ideas on who is after you?" Would he tell her?

"Take your pick. Could be a drug lord, weapons smugglers, terrorists…"

Okay, so that was probably the truth. Nobody would make up a list like that. The options were enough to give anyone heart palpitations, yet he was oddly nonchalant. Like a professional. He did know how to handle that gun. He was either a bad guy who'd ticked off some other bad guys, or a good guy with a lot of enemies. She decided to be optimistic. She desperately needed some hope to cling to, even if for only a few more moments. "You were in law enforcement?"

Say yes. Please say yes.

"Kind of."

Her nerves were as frayed as the cuffs of his jeans. "If you say *kind of* one more time, I'm going to scream."

"Nothing I haven't heard before," he said, humor glinting in his eyes.

He thought this was funny? The man lived to drive her crazy. Swear to God, if she had a grenade launcher…

She caught herself. She believed in a universe that could be influenced by positive and negative thoughts. In the situation she was in, there was no sense thinking violent thoughts. She closed her eyes for a moment and briefly envisioned getting away from the man.

He pulled into the parking lot of a diner, which, unlike the post office lot, looked fairly full.

DeDe's was a plain, square clapboard building that never made it into visitors' guides. Tourists who came to Chadds Ford to discover the country's colonial past wouldn't have looked at it twice, anyway. But the food was divine, which made it a favorite meeting place for locals. She used to have breakfast here with her grandmother every Sunday, before she'd passed.

She closed her eyes for a moment and drew a deep breath. "What are we doing here?"

"Getting breakfast." He was checking out the lot carefully.

"How can you eat at a time like this?"

He shrugged. "If you don't eat, you won't have the strength to face whatever comes next."

He had a very pragmatic view of eating. Judging from his lean body, he'd never spent a day of his life overeating, or dieting, or wrought with emotion that made ice cream a necessity, for that matter. "I don't think I can eat right now."

"You can always give it a try. A sandwich and orange juice?"

"Okay. And coffee." Although if there were ever a morning when she was wide-awake without caffeine, this would be it. Still, old habits died harder than Duracell batteries. And caffeine wasn't just about waking up. It was her comfort food of choice. Among others. Suddenly she could have killed for a bag of Cheetos.

Not that there was a chance of getting Cheetos out of Cade. She'd seen his grocery bags before—he was a health nut. He shopped at Trader Joe's.

"You stay here." He scanned the parking lot one more time before starting out. "I'll get it to go."

She watched him walk to the front door and hold it open for a group of old ladies. He trusted her to stay put. He really had seemed competent until now. So competent that she was beginning to feel dejected about her chances of getting away from him. *Well, everybody makes mistakes.*

She was out of the SUV the second the door closed behind him. And she nearly got run over by the cop car pulling into the lot.

HE THOUGHT HE'D LOST Palmer, but spotted him in that SUV by accident and thanked his lucky stars for it. Luck had always been on his side. And why not? Luck favored the prepared mind. Wasn't that what they said? And he always was prepared.

So was Cade Palmer, it seemed. He'd escaped that explosion. That had been a surprise in the middle of his morning surveillance. He'd been checking out the house, making his own plans. He wouldn't have minded if someone else took care of Palmer. He wasn't vain that way, didn't take his business personally like some others he knew—no sense in that. Whatever way the man was rubbed out was fine with him.

As he had stalked closer, he'd watched the woman Palmer left in the car. He wanted Palmer, but he could settle for her now. Palmer would come after her—he could never resist saving everyone in sight and then some. He would have grabbed her were it not for the damn cop who came at the worst moment, when he was a few feet from the Escalade and she was looking in the opposite direction, not having a clue.

He did have time to notice her nice legs. He wasn't averse to bonuses. That Palmer had likely had her already didn't detract from her charms—maybe it even added to them. He'd enjoy taking something that was Palmer's.

But he couldn't risk her making any noise now, couldn't afford even a momentary struggle. He pulled back into the cover of his own vehicle. He could wait. He had waited for months already, never knowing where the bastard was, never knowing if he was going to wake to Palmer's gun pressed to his forehead.

He had the man's scent now, was on his trail. He would get him in the end. He always got his man. That was how he had stayed alive in parts of the world where violence was an everyday occurrence and respected businessmen and politicians went to dinner with assassins and murderers.

He couldn't say he liked the life, but he understood it and was good at it, had achieved a measure of success fishing in those murky waters. He wasn't about to let Cade Palmer take that away from him. And one thing was clear. With the past they shared, it would always come down to kill or be killed between the two of them.

Palmer was good at killing.

But he was better.

CADE STUDIED THE POSTED menu, turning his cell phone over in his hand. He was supposed to meet Abhi in half an hour. Had the man betrayed him? He'd been the SDDU's trusted man in Jodhpur. But people switched sides all the time. No one knew that better than he did. The name David Smith tasted bitter on his tongue. Cade gripped his phone, irritated that the man at the front of the line was taking forever to order.

Abhi might know that he was alive. He had to consider that possibility. He had contacted the man under an assumed name, but Abhi had connections. He would dig deep before agreeing to a meet. Cade hadn't thought he could dig deep enough to get to him, but what if he had?

But even if Abhi had discovered his identity, he still wouldn't know where he lived. Cade couldn't see any possible way how the man could have found that out. Still, at one point Abhi had worked for BAKIN—Indonesian intelligence—which had since been restructured into BIN, the Badan Intelijen Negara. The man was scary good. A great guy to know as long as he was on your side. And therein lay the gamble.

He couldn't go to Abhi with Bailey in tow, and he couldn't leave Bailey behind. The question was whether to call Abhi and set another time for their meeting. If he didn't show, would Abhi pack up and go back to his Jodhpur hideout, taking his information with him? Probably not, not for a few days, not with the amount of money Cade had put on the table for information on David Smith.

He slipped his phone back into his pocket. He had to get Bailey out of the cross fire and hand her over to the authorities for safekeeping. But first he had to figure out why the FBI wanted them in the first place, and convince the Bureau that she didn't have anything to do with anything. He needed time, and he needed to find out which of his enemies had orchestrated this morning's attack—and how they had found him.

PERFECT. NICE TO HAVE some luck for a change. Bailey relaxed for the first time that morning. She smoothed her T-shirt down, tugged her hair into place and straightened her spine.

The black-and-white rolled into a parking space a few feet to her right. She walked toward it, wincing as the gravel scratched her bare feet. With a little more luck, she'd be given a ride home.

Not that she had shoes at home.

Not that she had a home. The thought took the air out of her lungs. She paused to catch her breath. Cade's craziness had distracted her from the fact that her house was gone. Why was it so hard to breathe? Her eyes burned.

She couldn't fall apart. Not yet. Not yet. She had to ask for help.

The nice officer was going to take her someplace safe where she could call her brother. They would let her wait at the police station until he came to pick her up. They would wrap her in a blanket and give her hot coffee. She watched TV—she knew how it went.

She would be told that it had been a gas explosion after all. *Grenade launcher. Right.* Could be that Cade was a crazy maniac who had blown up the house himself and concocted the whole story so she would willingly go with him.

What did she know about him, anyway? He'd lived in the house for only three months. He claimed to be Frank Garey's nephew, but she'd known Frank for nearly seven years and the retired truck driver had never mentioned any relatives to her.

She glanced toward the diner's entrance. A young couple came out, hugging and kissing for all they were worth, acting like they were madly in love. Bailey wasn't sold on the idea of love. Both sets of grandparents had divorced before she'd been born. Her parents' divorce was a mess she just as soon not think about. And now her brother's marriage had fallen under the ax.

The lovebirds outside the diner moved on without letting each other go for a second.

She couldn't see Cade. So far so good.

He would be mad as hell when he found her gone.

And she didn't want to see Cade Palmer mad. She'd seen him annoyed, and that was scary enough. In a few minutes, she would be under the protection of the law, safe from him and whatever was really going on.

Maybe they would never see each other again. That would be good. Bailey was pretty convinced that he was running from the law—otherwise he would have called the police after his house blew up. If fortune smiled on her, he would just keep running and never look back.

She stepped gingerly on the hot, sharp blacktop, running on nerves as she approached the cop car. The officer inside was shutting off the engine and fiddling with the laptop on the dashboard. Computer technology had entered every aspect of life these days. Even she had experimented with some digital garden-art designs, and thanks to her nephew's tips, had actually gotten better at it.

Deep breath. She needed a moment to collect her thoughts so she could explain her situation coherently and the policeman wouldn't think her a raving lunatic. She finger-combed her tangled hair one more time. *Hi. My house exploded this morning.* She bit her lip. How about *Hi. I was kidnapped?* Would that be putting it too strongly? Cade had said he only wanted to protect her. He'd done nothing to harm her so far—but he did have a gun. She filled her lungs with air again.

She could see the screen and the scrolling images on the officer's laptop. As she tried to figure out what she would say to him once he stepped out of the car,

Cade's picture flashed on, with a single line of text on top. She moved closer to read it, but the picture changed too quickly.

She stared, rooted to the spot, as her own image scrolled onto the screen.

Where did they get *that?*

Her attention was quickly drawn from last year's much-regretted experimental perm to the bolded message above her photo.

WANTED BY THE FBI. And below that, another line: CONSIDERED ARMED AND DANGEROUS.

Chapter Three

Damn. She was going for the cop. Couldn't be left alone for a minute. Cade had looked back through the windows just in the nick of time.

"Excuse me." He pushed through the people in line behind him, stepped outside and walked toward her as fast as he could without drawing attention. She seemed to be hesitating.

"How many bagels did you say you wanted, babe?"

She startled and whipped around, with a stunned look on her face, and hesitated for another beat as she glanced back at the black-and-white—hesitated too long.

"You better look at their choices." He grabbed her by the elbow in what looked like an intimate gesture but would have been impossible to shake off had she tried, and steered her toward the diner, growling only two short words under his breath. "Get inside."

A waitress hurried by just as they stepped in. "Good morning. Would you like a table?" Her smile didn't reach her tired eyes, her mind clearly someplace else. She was in her fifties but her shoulders sloped like someone decades older. She did not, thank God, notice Bailey's bare feet and point to the No Shoes, No Shirt, No Service sign on the door.

"Just picking up. Thanks." Cade headed to the take-out station once again, where a high-school kid was manning the counter. The line had disappeared while he'd gone to stop Bailey from making his life even more complicated than it already was.

"Hi. One cup of coffee with all the fixings." He'd seen the syrupy stuff Bailey carried around all day long in her "Gardens are Art" oversize mug.

The kid grabbed a purple DeDe's plastic coffee cup. "Anything else?"

Cade let go of Bailey's elbow and draped an arm casually around her slim waist, ignoring the kaleidoscope of donuts with their colored frosting in the antique display case in front of him. "Two breakfast sandwiches on whole-wheat bagels. Two bottles of orange juice." His body was a weapon—he didn't put junk into it any more than he would have shoved sand down his rifle barrel.

"Fifteen sixty-five."

He put a twenty on the counter. "Keep the change."

"Thank you, sir." The kid's smile widened, and he put some spring in his step as he went to get their food.

He was handing Cade the bag when the cop came in. Cade watched the man for a moment from the corner of his eye. The officer sat at a corner table and buried his head in the breakfast menu.

"Thanks." Cade grabbed their food while Bailey reached for her coffee.

"Thank you for stopping in. Have a great day. Good morning. What can I get you today, sir?" The kid was already serving the next customer.

Cade didn't have a free hand to hang on to Bailey, so he did his best to herd her in front of him before she got another brilliant idea. Especially since the cop was done making his selection and was scanning the place for the nearest waitress.

Cade watched Bailey for signs that she was ready to bolt, but she'd been uncharacteristically quiet since he'd brought her into the diner. He moved between her and the cop to block his view, turning his back.

Once they were at the door, he checked out the parking lot before stepping out, scanning the cars and the man who had just pulled in before walking to the Escalade.

"Don't do that again." He didn't raise his voice but made sure his tone conveyed his message sufficiently.

She bit her lip and tightened her grip on her coffee.

Was he scaring her yet? He sure as hell hoped so. He hoped he could scare her enough to stop her from doing something colossally stupid. She looked subdued, if not scared. That was something.

"Help yourself." He put the food between them once they got into the car, but he didn't touch his. He wanted to be a little farther down the road—and in a different car—first.

He glanced into the rearview mirror before backing

out of his spot and saw the cop at the diner's door, looking at the cars in the parking lot. Time to haul ass.

He pulled out onto Route 1 but veered off almost immediately onto a side street. He snaked through a labyrinth of housing developments. Maybe the cop was looking for the Escalade. Whoever owned it could easily have called it in by now.

Bailey sipped her coffee, set it in the cup holder and looked at him, anxiety in her eyes. "I understand that you think you are saving me, but I'm asking you to let me go. Please."

She still didn't get it. "No."

Her jaw muscles tightened and her fists clenched. "I'm not going to quit trying to get away from you. You can't watch me every second. You are going to have to sleep at some point."

That was what she thought. He could go without rest for days when on a mission. But it would help both of them if she stopped struggling every step of the way.

"This is for your own good." That sounded lame— she wasn't going to go for that.

And she didn't.

"I can decide what's for my own good!" she shouted, clearly at the end of her rope. "Why does the FBI want us?"

The what? He lifted an eyebrow. He hadn't told her about the FBI—there was no sense in getting her all worked up. He figured the shock of her house blowing up was enough for one day, considering she was a civilian.

She drew a deep breath, which pushed her breasts

against the T-shirt of his that she'd borrowed. "Our picture was on that officer's computer in his car."

So that was why she'd stopped in her tracks when she'd reached the black-and-white. Could be the cop had recognized them in the diner.

He hesitated only a moment before reaching his decision. It would be easier to tell her the truth and gain her cooperation than watch her every second of every day until he figured out what was going on. "We've been implicated in domestic terrorism. Both of us," he added for emphasis.

She went white and stared at him. "Why?" Her mouth closed and then opened again, but nothing else came out.

"You tell me."

She was slack jawed for another minute before speaking again. "But they're wrong. We can explain that it's a mistake, can't we? We just have to tell them that it's crazy. They can't have any proof. We have to go back and talk to someone."

She seemed determined to rush into disaster. A real babe in the woods.

Her eyes pleaded with him. "Listen to me. We can't run. This is probably the worst thing we could be doing."

The fact that she still didn't trust him after he'd spent his entire morning saving her curvaceous be-hind frustrated him beyond words. "How keen are you on a surfing holiday?"

"*What* are you talking about?"

"Think water and a board."

Her eyes widened. She swallowed. "They wouldn't do that to us. We are U.S. citizens. They can't interrogate us like that." But she sounded less than certain.

"You'd be surprised what gets done behind closed doors these days. At the very least, we'll be taken in for serious interrogation. We're talking days, at the minimum. They are not going to let us go until they figure out what's going on. I'd prefer to figure things out on my own, then go in once we're cleared."

"But we didn't do anything."

"And eventually they would figure that out. My worry is what would happen in the meantime."

"They can't have any evidence."

"They might now. Our house blew up."

"You said those were terrorists."

"There's a chance there won't be any witnesses to testify to that. But the Feds will be finding pieces of guns and traces of C4 all over the ruins."

Again, no words came out of her mouth, which was still opening and closing as if she were a fish out of water. Which she was.

He shrugged. "Don't make a big deal out of this. They were left over from my old job."

"You had guns and explosives in the house?" she squeaked.

He glanced at her to make sure she was okay. "For self-protection."

She buried her face in her hands, leaning forward as far as the seat belt would allow. A full minute passed before she looked at him again, and it was clear from the set of her jaw how much effort it took for her to keep herself under control. "I could go back and tell them all that stuff was yours. You could hide until you clear yourself. I have nothing to do with any of this."

"Probably true. But do you think they'll take your word for it?"

That gave her something to think about for another minute or two. "Okay. But if we have to hide out while whatever this is gets resolved, I'd prefer to hide out on my own. That's my bottom line." She drew herself straight and tried to look very tough and businesslike. All five feet five inches of her. In silk pajama shorts, with no shoes, pink toenails wiggling furiously under the dashboard.

He bit back a grin. Gotta give the girl points for trying. "Where?"

"With my brother. Or a trusted friend."

He didn't miss the emphasis on *trusted*. "They'll have that covered."

The toe wiggling stopped. Her face went pale again. "You think they'll investigate my family?"

"Family, friends, coworkers. Consider it already done."

"But this is insane. This is so unfair."

Was it? He'd invaded people's privacy without a second thought if he'd determined that the information he could gain would move his mission forward. He hadn't given much thought to what it felt like from the other end. Didn't care much, truthfully. The kind of people who'd made it on to his radar screen were the kind of people who wouldn't hesitate to shoot a grenade through his house. "Welcome to the real world."

"Surreal world." She looked out the window at the peaceful community he was driving through, carefully obeying the speed limit. "What are we doing here?"

"Looking for another ride."

"You can't keep stealing. That *is* a crime. I don't want to get involved in things like this." There was a new edge of desperation in her voice.

He said nothing as he drove by house after house.

"Are you looking for something specific?" she snapped, shoving her cinnamon hair out of her face, giving him that furious fairy look.

He'd been developing a fascination with furious fairies in the past three months.

"A way out of here. This is a residential area. As soon as someone looks out their window, they'll notice if their car is gone. I need a business where people won't go out into the parking lot again at least until their lunch break." He turned onto a bigger road at the end of the street and saw some office buildings not far off. He headed that way.

"Do you do this a lot?"

He thought back to other cars he'd borrowed on various undercover missions. And that one plane, an older model Cessna, in Colombia. "When necessary."

She groaned.

"Drink your coffee." Those full lips needed an occupation other than nagging. He could have suggested a number of activities for them that would have made him happy. Damn, if he looked at her long enough, he could almost feel her lips on him. But based on the killer look she was shooting him at the moment, it probably wasn't the right time to suggest anything…personal.

"I'm fully awake. Thanks," she said, crossing her arms over her chest and blocking his view of her nipples as they pushed against the fabric of his T-shirt. He sure did love air-conditioning.

He navigated over to the corporate park and stopped. "Okay, let's go."

"This is a bus stop."

"They'll find the car and get it back to the owner faster if we leave it here." He waited until she got out and then swung his bag over his shoulder, picked up her pajama top from the back and wiped the interior and the door handles to remove fingerprints. "Hey, that's mine," she protested, grabbing at the top.

"It can be washed. You just said you didn't want to be linked to things like grand theft auto." He gave her a pointed look. "Let's not leave a calling card."

"You're so good at this, it's scary." She watched him through narrowed eyes. "I suppose if you weren't, you'd be in jail," she added.

If he weren't, he'd be dead.

A quick scan of the parking lot turned up exactly what he wanted: a Land Rover with four-wheel drive. The doors were locked, but he had his bag of tricks with him. He reached in and pulled out a small tool kit.

In minutes, they were on the road, heading south. He didn't stop until they crossed the Maryland border, and then only long enough to run into Wal-Mart for a few changes of clothes, plus shoes for her, food and another canvas bag to stash everything in.

"When are you going to tell me where we're heading?" she asked when they were back on the road again, her fine legs covered by new, tan capri pants.

"A friend of mine has a fishing camp at one of the smaller lakes around here."

"We can't live at a fishing camp for the rest of our lives. We have to talk to someone. I really think you're making a mistake here."

Oddly, staying at the camp with her for a prolonged time didn't seem all that unappealing, despite her endless questioning of his judgment. He would just have to find another occupation for that smart mouth of hers.

"We're staying until we can figure out who is after me. Or you," he added, voicing a thought that had been idling in his mind since the Colonel had told him she was on the FBI's list, too. "Any enemies?"

She gave him her signature glare—annoyance fused with impatience and suffering—and turned her pixie nose way up in the air. "Don't be ridiculous."

He didn't think it likely that the tangos had anything to do with her, but until he had proof positive who the bastards were and what they wanted, he couldn't dismiss any possibility. And he couldn't let her go. Couldn't let her go, anyway, as long as the FBI was looking for her. If they had a bone to pick with him, he didn't want them to find her and drag her into his mess.

He recognized the turnoff and took it. Ten miles later, he found himself in a maze of small, unpaved roads, gravel crunching under the tires. He'd only been to Joey's camp once, ten years ago. The area had changed since—it was built up, with hardly any open land left. New drives and lanes had been put in.

"Lost?" she asked when he rolled down the same street the second time around.

"Canvassing the neighborhood before approaching the target."

The look on her face told him he wasn't fooling her. "Too bad we don't have GPS."

"I wouldn't have taken the car if it did. We could have been tracked through that."

"Do you always think of everything?" She sounded more annoyed than impressed.

And why in hell would that bother him? He wasn't trying to impress her. He just wanted to make sure that nothing bad happened to her, especially not because of his questionable past.

"I try." He flashed her a grin as he caught a familiar sight through the window.

Joey's place hadn't changed, except for a new tin roof. It was still just a shack for a weekend of beer drinking and fishing. Heaven.

"This is it?" she asked when he slowed. "You've got to be kidding."

"Home sweet home."

"I'll sleep in the car, if it's all the same to you. You go in, figure out what's going on, come out when you have it, and then we go home."

"We have to get rid of the car."

Pause. "Can't we just take off the license plate? Or cover it with something?"

"There's a chance that it might have LoJack." Technology worked both ways—sometimes it made life easier; sometimes it made life harder.

She closed her eyes for a moment. "Okay."

Not that he needed her approval or permission. The decisions would be made by him on this mission. Maybe she didn't fully grasp that yet. She would.

He drove the car to a small train station just as the train to Baltimore pulled in. Inspired by a sudden idea, he bought two tickets for the next train to New York from a ticket agent, and then called a tow truck from the public phone. He told the guy to tow the car to the Baltimore harbor parking lot and drop it off there.

If it had LoJack, the cops would follow it there. If any witnesses remembered the towing service's name and the cops asked the guy where the pickup had been, they'd go to the train station and talk to the ticket agent, who would say he'd bought two tickets to New York. The cops would think he and Bailey had sent the car to Baltimore as a decoy and then gotten on the train to New York. That would make sense— her brother was there. He was sure the cops and Agent Rubliczky would make that assumption. *If* they connected Cade and Bailey to the stolen car at all. He felt reasonably safe to spend a few days at Joey's camp.

"And how are we going to get around?" she asked as the tow truck disappeared in the distance with a good chunk of his cash.

They were in the middle of nowhere. Next to the station was a garish gift-shop tent with "Final Sale" and "Everything $5" written all over it. He could see the lake glistening in the distance, could smell the water from here. The beach was a short walk away. People lay out on the sand and on boats. The path to the beach was clear; everyone who'd gotten off the train had already made their way down.

"We'll have ourselves a lovely stroll." He scanned the main road, which was just a few hundred feet from the station. "Or not," he said as a police cruiser appeared and took the damn turnoff. If the Land Rover was discovered missing shortly after he'd taken it, if it did have LoJack…. He glanced toward the lake, which was blue and brilliant and inviting. "How about a swim?"

Her eyes went wide as she took a step back from him. "I can't swim."

"At all?" Everybody knew how to swim. Who didn't know how to swim? A woman whose middle name was Trouble, that was who.

Annoyance filled her blue-violet eyes. "I work at a garden center. I don't need to know how to swim. The biggest body of water I ever see is the indoor lily pond."

"Take it easy," he said under his breath, taking stock of their situation.

His bag was slung over his shoulder, covering the gun tucked into his waistband at the small of his back. Bailey carried the canvas bag with the clothes and food. With a little help, they could look like tourists.

Thank God for the obligatory souvenir tent. He grabbed a My Fish Is Bigger Than Yours baseball hat with fake blond hair attached for her and a pair of dorky-looking sunglasses for himself along with two cheap fishing poles. He paid for them, and they headed straight for the path that led to the lake.

They would blend in with the people sunning and fishing on the shore unless the cops came in for a closer look, in which case they'd just have to keep moving.

Another cop car suddenly pulled in. To continue toward the lake would mean passing right by the police officer. But they had already started out on the path. To turn abruptly around would look suspicious.

He stopped, sneaked his arms around Bailey's slim waist and turned her to him.

She was scared enough not to protest. Blue-violet eyes searched his face. Her mouth was set in a tight line of fear. "They are going to catch us, aren't they? I don't know if I should hope for that or keep running from it. I don't know you—"

"I used to work for the Department of Homeland Security."

Her eyes widened. "Kind of?"

He bit back a grin. Yeah, kind of. His group, the SDDU, was a top secret commando team used for black ops. The unit's existence was known only to a select few, even at the highest reaches of government. Their leader, Colonel Wilson, reported directly to the secretary of Homeland Security.

"You're safe with me. Relax." He dipped his head

as the cop got out of his car. The man was heading toward the train station, toward them. There was only one way he could think of to cover their faces.

"I'm going to kiss you," he warned.

She looked too petrified to protest. Certainly too petrified to enjoy it. Too bad, because he planned on doing just that. He had stared at her full lips many times since he'd moved in, and had contemplated some serious lip-locking with his shrew of a neighbor. He could be annoyed with her and lust after her at the same time. The male mind was a marvel of biology, no mistake about it.

He brushed his lips over hers—full, sweet, soft— and swallowed a moan that began to bubble up inside his chest. No sense getting too worked up with a cop heading their way.

"It might help if you look like you're into this," he whispered against her mouth.

She relaxed marginally in his arms.

The cop was only a few feet from them and still coming.

Cade opened his mouth over hers. He was going to make this kiss look real—that was his last co- herent thought.

Their lips were doing all the touching, but it was his groin that got all the heat. Funny how that worked. He had expected pleasure—she was a fine- looking woman with a body that would have made any healthy man sit up and take notice. But he hadn't expected his breath to get caught in the middle of his chest. That didn't usually happen.

He went on a pilgrimage across her lower lip first, then the top. He tasted her, licked at the seam of her lips, kissed the corners of her mouth. Amazing how much more attractive that mouth was when she wasn't using it to yell at him, when he could feel its velvety softness against his own. He nuzzled her cheek, kissing her again and again.

His hand tightened on her waist, then slipped lower, one slow inch at a time. His mind was turning into mush—an interesting contrast to the definite hardening that was going on below. And she still hadn't responded yet.

He reluctantly pulled away.

And he realized that the cop had not only passed by them but had gone into the station without him noticing. Not good.

She looked a little off balance, but not overwhelmed with pleasure and driving need. And even the off-balance thing could have been because of the cop.

That didn't sit well with his self-esteem.

"Okay. Let's go while we can," she said.

Okay?

He badly wanted a rematch. A chance to prove to her that she wasn't as immune to him as she thought, to kiss her until she begged for what he'd been about ready to beg for a moment ago. But he recognized the notion for what it was—a huge distraction from their mission and a danger to his concentration. Which meant that for the duration, he would not—could not—kiss or touch Bailey Preston again.

HE WAS CRAZY. JUST absolutely certifiable. Bailey stepped back, not daring to look at him.

He was also sexy, with a body to die for and lips that had mesmerized her without half trying. He'd made her head spin, but she was too far gone with nerves to respond to him. Thank God for small mercies. She took another step away from him, needing to put some space between them before the shock wore off and her knees gave way.

He was looking at her funny. He cleared his throat. "Yeah, we better get out of here." Taking her hand, he headed toward the lake.

She didn't pull away, even if the thought of spending time in that small shack with him seriously scared her. Now more than ever. Even if she was inclined to believe what he had said about the DHS. He'd clearly had some sort of training. She'd nearly asked if he had any sort of ID to back up his claim and then remembered the stack of fake IDs she'd seen in his bag. Even if he had something with DHS on it, it wouldn't mean a thing.

"You said you used to work for the DHS?"

"Retired."

He didn't look old enough to be retired. He was pretty much the most virile man she'd ever known. Her doubts must have shown on her face.

"Due to injury," he said.

And she remembered the scars she'd seen on his back when he'd mowed the lawn sans T-shirt. She'd asked the first time she'd seen them. "Motorcycle accident," he had said. Slid on his back, road scraped off his skin. No big deal.

Uh-huh. Tell me another one.

He held her gaze with those caramel eyes, fringed with thick, dark lashes, as if whether she believed him or not mattered.

And the weird thing was, she did. Because deep down, she couldn't believe that he was an evil man. Annoying at times, yes. But he was also the guy who had climbed the roof in the middle of a thunderstorm to rescue Mrs. Kuzimo's kitten. The guy who mowed her lawn every single time, without having been asked. "No big deal, I'm out here with this noise box, anyway," he'd say. The guy who cleared the leaves from her gutters before she noticed they were plugged. The guy who… "Okay. You're one of the good guys."

"Let's not go overboard." But he was grinning.

Which drew her attention to his lips again.

"You kissed me." The stunned thought that had been circling in the back of her head somehow slipped through her still-tingling lips.

He shrugged. The grin stayed. "No big deal. We're kissing neighbors."

If he could make light of it, so could she. "Is that like kissing cousins?"

His grin widened into a breathtaking spectacle of delicious lips and white teeth. His voice dropped to a suggestive, husky tone when he said, "It's much, much better."

Oh, my.

Her life was now officially completely out of control—not just what went on outside her, but what went on inside her as well. Which was the real scary part. She'd lost her mind. If she hadn't, she wouldn't be wishing that Cade would kiss her again.

She needed to change the subject.

"How long do you think we'll be staying here?"

"I don't want to stay too long in one place. I need to make some calls and I need a computer with an Internet connection. Might have to contact some old friends." The grin slid off his face. "Not that I want to drag anyone else into this."

They walked the upper edge of the beach, keeping their distance from the sun worshippers and everyone else.

"Do they have Internet around here?" Those fishing huts hadn't looked too high tech.

"There's bound to be an Internet café in town."

"Haven't seen a town."

"It's a few miles down the shore."

"I guess we'll be walking a lot." She wished they could have kept the car. She felt safer in a vehicle, less exposed.

"Walking is good exercise."

He didn't seem to be too put out by their situation, as if he played the hiding-out game all the time. He probably did, now that she thought about it.

"Are you going to tell me any more about yourself?" She could have come up with a hundred questions or so without breaking a sweat.

"No."

Through his shirt, she caught sight of the gun he'd tucked into his waistband. He was way out of her league. So far out, most likely, that she wasn't even fully realizing yet how much trouble she was in.

"Would you have to kill me if you did? When they say that in movies, is that for real? Because I can stop pushing."

He glanced at her sideways and grinned. He really was unfairly sexy. "Watch spy thrillers much?"

"Now and again."

"I have no plans to hurt you."

Which, she noted, was not the same as saying he *wasn't* going to hurt her. Then again, he had told her before that he didn't like making promises he couldn't keep.

He must have read the doubt in her eyes. "I'm trying to protect you. I'm not sure if I'm one of the good guys exactly the way you mean it, but I do have some principles, such as they are."

And she had to accept that was as much reassurance as she was going to get from the man. "I'll just think of you as a kind of good guy with a gun and principles." She had to put her faith in the benevolence of the universe.

He flashed another grin.

"God, I need to get out and meet new people," she groaned.

They walked on in the sand, which went right in the toes of her sandals, so every few steps or so she had to hobble around to shake it out. But she knew that was the least of her problems.

"I have to get in touch with my brother. He's going through a bad divorce." Trampled on and broken-hearted. She'd warned him about the mass hysteria that greeting card companies and Hollywood script-writers called love. He'd been too far gone to listen. The least she could do now was to be there for him and for Zak. "He'll be looking for me. I don't want him worried. You have to let me make at least a quick call. And I do have a job. And a business."

"Just not for a few more days." He let her hand go once they were out of sight of the train station.

She flexed her fingers, then wrapped her arms around her chest, annoyed at herself for missing that connection. Whatever he said about wanting only to protect her, she had to remember just how little she really knew about him.

"Right." A few more days. In the company of a gun-toting kind of good guy with principles. On the run from the FBI and possibly some terrorists. She wasn't going to think about that part. She was going to grab hold of the "with principles" part and hang on to that.

They passed the rest of the walk in silence. He was probably planning the details of their impossible mission. She was just trying to hold herself together and not start sobbing.

They were near the shack when they spotted the cruiser rolling down the dirt road, going slowly, checking out the row of weekend bungalows.

"Cade?" She looked at him. They had absolutely no place to go. Cops ahead, water behind.

They were so doomed. Suddenly, doubts rose by the dozen, smothering her. They never should have run in the first place. Taking off made everything so much worse, making them look like they had something to hide. She shouldn't have left with him. Should have fought him tooth and nail, should have screamed bloody murder, should have—at the very least—given herself up to the cop in DeDe's parking lot.

An FBI interrogation. She swallowed the Ping-Pong ball in her throat. Her nerve endings buzzed with sheer terror as she watched the cop car, unable to look away from it. She felt like a fish caught in a net, all tangled up with no way out. His hand on her arm brought her attention back to him, distracting her from impending doom for a split second.

His intense caramel eyes searched her face. "Do you trust me?" he asked.

Chapter Four

"No," Bailey said without thinking. "Not at all. Absolutely not." In fact, she was beginning to rue the day she'd ever set eyes on the man.

A frown creased his forehead. "Don't you think that's overkill? A single *no* would have done. A *maybe* would have been nice."

She blinked. Like, what—she'd hurt his feelings? She had bigger things to worry about.

"Come on." He walked away from her, his steps full of purpose.

Apparently, at least one of them thought he knew what he was doing.

Trust or no trust, she followed him. He *had* proven himself competent so far. And he had gotten her out of the house before it blew. Someday she was going to thank him for that. Right now she couldn't bear thinking about it. She couldn't face the fact that the home she had worked so hard for was gone.

He sneaked up to the lean-to behind his friend's

fishing shack and pulled out a two-seater canoe. "Grab the end."

She had a bad feeling about this but did as he asked—ordered, really. The man had to work on his people skills. But it didn't seem like the best time to point that out to him.

He picked up the other end and two paddles. "I'll go first," he said as he headed for the water. "The goal is to always keep something between us and the cops."

Since they'd been pretty close to shore in the first place, it didn't take them long to reach the water. The beach ended a hundred or so feet to the left, and there was little sand on the shore. A long dock reached into the water, used by fishermen. The lake seemed endless, the other side barely visible.

Her hands tingled with nerves. She consoled herself with the fact that the sky was clear. "Have I mentioned that I can't swim?" Could be it slipped his mind. Or maybe he was just going to float the canoe out to the middle of the lake and blow it up to draw the cops' attention. She could only hope.

"You won't have to," he said, looking over his shoulder.

There. He wouldn't make her go out on the lake. Maybe he really was a nice guy. Maybe she had misjudged him. She gave him a semi-smile of appreciation.

"Just take care not to fall in," he said, looking over his shoulder.

The urge to yell at him took effort to suppress. It helped that her fear overpowered her anger. "Don't these things tip easily?"

He put the canoe in the water. "Not today. I'll hold it. Step in and sit down. While we are out there, whatever happens, don't stand up."

"Okay." That wasn't hard to promise. She pretty much figured she'd be frozen to her seat.

A compassionate universe wouldn't let her drown. She fixed that thought in her mind and held on to it. *Cade* wouldn't let her drown. Oddly, that thought seemed just as—if not more—comforting as the first. She was in real bad shape if she was starting to put her trust in Cade Palmer, annoying and hot neighbor extraordinaire.

Just watching the waves lick the canoe's side made her nervous. Last chance to back out.

She glanced toward the cop car that was canvassing the narrow lanes, stopping to talk to people. *FBI interrogation.* "Okay, let's do it," she said and didn't stop to think how crazy it was that she would trust Cade more than she trusted the benevolence of the universe or, for that matter, the checks and balances of her own government.

He helped her into the back, then strode into the water to put in their bags before sitting down in front of her and handing her one of the paddles. "Relax."

"Shouldn't we have life vests on?" The pronounced lack of life-saving devices made it very hard for her to "relax."

"Weren't any in the shed."

Weren't those things mandatory? Why didn't his friend have them? Obviously, he had irresponsible friends. Why wasn't she surprised? Maybe she should reevaluate her newfound trust in the man.

"Watch what I do and do the same. It's not hard to pick up the rhythm." He pushed away and dipped his paddle into the water on his right, obviously unconcerned about a cold and watery grave.

Then they were away from the shore, moving rapidly, gliding across the surface of the water with each push of his powerful arms. She ignored the goose bumps of unease that spread across her skin and copied him movement for movement. And for a while she was so focused, that she forgot to worry about getting farther and farther away from shore.

But then she looked back and registered how far out they were, how deep the water must be, how the waves splashed against the canoe's side.… Her arms stopped. *Can't, can't, can't. Oh, God.* She wanted to get back to firm ground, but she couldn't even move to paddle back. A helicopter rescue would have been really nice. Just lift her right out. Snug in a harness. Please.

"Take it easy. Try to focus on something else," he said without turning back.

Easy for him to say. But after a moment, she calmed herself enough to focus on his wide shoulders, the only thing in her line of vision other than water. Strong and close enough to grab on to in case of emergency. "How far do we have to go?" She hated the mousy squeak in her voice. Sweat beaded above her lip. At least he couldn't see that.

"Not far. Just over there." His voice was patient,

his tone deep and calming. He motioned with his head toward a sizable patch of reeds.

If there were reeds there, the water had to be fairly shallow. This thought set her at ease a bit. "How long do we have to stay out here?"

"Not long. There's a storm coming."

She clenched her paddle tighter. "What storm?" There wasn't a cloud in the sky, the wind picking up only a little.

But by the time they reached the reeds, the first clouds appeared from the east. Within half an hour it was raining. Another fifteen minutes after that, a summer storm was beating them with full force.

"Keep down."

Like she had to be told. She huddled in her seat, shivering as he pulled the canoe to the edge of the reeds, close enough so they could see out while still remaining hidden. The beach was already empty. The last of the fishermen were going to shore. A cop car was parked by the dock, two police officers checking out everyone who was coming in.

"Here. Give me your paddle." He took it from her and laid it in the canoe. "See if you can scoot closer without upsetting the balance."

She inched forward, while holding her breath, until their bodies touched. His wet shirt did little to diminish the heat that radiated from his back, and she snuggled up to him, putting her arms around his waist after a moment, wanting to be even closer, his warmth feeling so good as rain pelted her back.

Then he executed some slick maneuver, and the

next thing she knew he was turned around, holding her in his arms. Being pressed against him like this, in the shelter of his wide chest, his head bowed over hers, her face pressed against the strong column of his neck, made the lake seem less threatening somehow, the storm quieter, the wind not as merciless. She clung to him, forgetting pride and propriety, appreciating the comfort he offered.

"You really think we're in this much trouble?" she said into his soaked shirt collar. He was taking some pretty extraordinary measures.

"Picture your house the last time you saw it."

She shuddered. He was right.

She clung to him in the storm, the reality of her situation seeping in slowly until she was numb not only with cold but with the weight of the quandary she found herself in. Up until now, she had led an ordinary life. Boring even. Exciting and terrifying things tended to happen to her brother, who'd hitchhiked through South America one summer break from UCLA and nearly gotten kidnapped by guerillas. Then, once he'd received his degree, he'd moved to Manhattan to marry a wealthy socialite, where he rubbed elbows with the rich and famous, and witnessed the horror of 9/11.

She'd gone to a local college, got a local job, dated and broken up with local men and bought a house locally when she'd finally squirreled away enough for a down payment. The sad truth was that Cade Palmer was the most exciting thing that had ever happened to her. She spent some time contemplating how pathetic that was. As soon as she was out of mortal danger, she was going to come up with a brand-new life plan.

When the lake was empty of boats and the cops had left, Cade waited another ten minutes and then decided that they could finally paddle out. When they reached the dock, he got out first and helped her to shore, holding her hand maybe a fraction of a second longer than necessary. She flushed with embarrassment, thinking how she'd clung to him in the reeds.

She wouldn't be doing herself any favors by denying that she was rapidly falling in lust with the man. She thanked her lucky stars that she didn't believe in falling in love. She was safe, at least, from that.

"We should probably get out of this weather." She bent to pick up the canoe, and they carried it back to the lean-to over their heads, using it as an umbrella. No cops in sight.

He reached up to the rafters after they set the canoe down, searched around and came up with a key. He flashed her a smile, which for a second made her forget how cold she was. Whatever else could be said about the man, he did have devastating eyes and an equally devastating smile. Odd that he hadn't had any female visitors in the three months since he had moved in. No visitors at all, in fact. Of course, considering his difficult personality, perhaps that was understandable. And then there was his job with the DHS.

"If you used to work for the government, why were you hiding from the authorities in Chadds Ford?" she asked.

"I wasn't hiding from the authorities."

"But you were hiding." Now she was getting somewhere.

He considered her for a moment. "From my past."

From the bad guys in his past, like the ones who blew their house up. She could still barely process that.

"What does the FBI want from you?" Then she added, on second thought, "From us?"

"When I figure that out, you'll be the first to know."

That part made no sense whatsoever. "A case of mistaken identities, you think?"

He shrugged. "Anything's possible."

He opened the front door and showed her into a ten-by-ten room. Her previous line of questioning was immediately forgotten. Judging from the dust and the cobwebs, whoever his friend was hadn't gotten a lot of fishing done so far this summer.

She was about to remark on that when she noticed he was staring at her in a strange way.

"What?"

His gaze snapped back into focus. "Sorry." He seemed to shake off whatever had gotten hold of him. "Kitchen." He pointed toward the electric hot plate on top of a dresser next to a small fridge. "Living room." He walked toward a sofa that had seen better days and opened it. "Bedroom." It wasn't a sofa, after all, but a futon. "And bathroom." He indicated a folding plastic door, with a proud grin. "What do you think?"

"Mother of God, have mercy," she said. "'When did I have my last tetanus shot?' comes in as a close second."

One dark eyebrow lifted. "Hey, you have a sense of humor."

She was instantly annoyed. Had he thought her as bad as that? That hurt, especially since her opinion of him had been improving. She drew herself up straight. What he thought of her didn't matter.

"Excuse me," she said, with all the dignity she could muster, and marched the two steps to the bathroom. She needed to put some distance between them and reestablish personal boundaries. A hot bath would give her time, stave off a cold and undoubtedly put her in a better mood.

She struggled with the folding door, won and stood gaping.

The best thing that could be said for the bathroom was that it had a door. The space was incredibly small. And she was pretty sure she was the first woman it had ever seen. One bar of dried-out soap. No bath. No shower. Just a bowl on a stand.

Her gaze caught on the small, streaked wall mirror, and she jumped in, yanking the door closed behind her. She'd been sleeping when Cade had broken into her bedroom, and hadn't had a bra on. She'd bought one at Wal-Mart but had been hoping for some privacy to put it on. She'd waited too long. The rain had soaked the white T-shirt she'd borrowed from him, plastering it to her torso, leaving nothing to the imagination.

She grabbed the single towel and rubbed the front of her shirt. She had dry clothes in the "living room" but she wasn't going out there like this. She'd sit

here until the damn shirt dried if she had to. She did
the best she could with the towel and then turned her
mind to other business.

The toilet. The seat wasn't down. Because the
toilet didn't have a seat. She flushed, grateful that at
least the plumbing was working. The tap trickled
cold water only. The sink had enough hard-water
stains for a Rorschach test.

She stared at them for a moment, suddenly overwhelmed with exhaustion. As she stared, the stains
began to take shape. If she didn't know any better
she'd think she was seeing her own doom.

CADE HAD JUST FINISHED prying up the floorboard
under the futon when she came out, hair somewhat
tamed, face freshly scrubbed. Her lips were forced
into the usual disapproving line, but they weren't
fooling him. Bailey Preston had a lush, sweet mouth.

The memory of their pretend kiss shot straight to
his groin. Again. Always. That seemed to be a pretty
dependable repeat effect with her. Maybe that had
always been the trouble, the source of the tension
between them. She was a beautiful woman with a
great body. He was a man. Having to listen to her
shower run on the other side of the wall every night
and knowing she was just feet from him, naked, was
enough to make any man a little nuts.

And he could absolutely not put the moves on
her, because he didn't know how long he would have
to hide out. Or where he would end up when the dust
settled. He didn't do long-term relationships, and a

fling with someone who lived next door was out of the question. Not that they lived next door to each other anymore. But she'd been hell to live with as it was. He hated to think what she would be like if they got together and then split.

"What are you doing?" she asked in her trademark, full-of-censure voice, which would have been easy to hate if it didn't have that underlying tone of sultry sensuality that drove him mad on a regular basis.

Her T-shirt was nearly dry. Disappointing. But better for their mission. This way, he had a shot at getting his raging lust under control. Having her practically sit on his lap in that canoe had seriously tested his willpower.

"Now that the view has been obscured, I'm checking out emergency supplies."

If looks could kill, he would have been flatlining.

He glanced toward the window. "Can't see anything through this rain. I don't think the cops will be coming back, though." He pulled a Beretta, three boxes of 9 mm bullets and finally a hand grenade from the hole. "Can you shoot a gun?"

"What do you think?" she snapped.

He put the Beretta back and covered the hole again. "Then you're safer without one." He pushed the futon into place and put the bullets and the hand grenade into his bag.

"I'm going to make some calls." He pulled out his phone. "I'm hungry." He looked at the bag that held the food they'd gotten earlier. "Maybe you could cook something after you change. You should really get out of those wet clothes."

Her face turned an interesting shade of red, her pixie nose going straight up in the air, but she grabbed some clothes out of the bag and headed back to the bathroom with them.

He dialed the Colonel, a man he trusted like few others. "Anything new, sir?"

"You've been traced to New York."

"Not a problem, sir."

"I didn't think so. Agent Rubliczky is foaming at the mouth. Any worse and he'll need a rabies shot. Some communications have been traced to your computer. I'm working on finding out what they were about. Care to give me a hint?"

"No idea, sir." He hadn't been involved in anything remotely interesting in the past three months. He'd been researching possibilities for the security agency he'd thought about opening when the inactivity of retirement eventually got to him. He'd tracked David Smith in other ways, making sure that nothing would ever point back to him. He'd been careful to contact Abhi through a secure chat room, using a PC at the Newark public library in Delaware.

"So they found my laptop?" He really wished he'd been able to get that out.

Bailey emerged from the bathroom in a striped, sleeveless shirt and shorts, looking good enough to eat. He had to get his mind off her perfect breasts and the way they'd felt pressed against his chest in that canoe. She showed no sign of lingering over any of that. And she had a bra on. He came close to sighing in disappointment. She was marching off to the hot plate, muttering something under her breath.

"Melted to a blob," the Colonel was saying.

Looking at her toned legs, Cade could relate to the concept of melting. Being around her raised his core temperature a notch—his clothes were already dry.

"It didn't improve Rubliczky's mood," the Colonel went on. "But they did find another computer, which seems to have a salvageable hard drive. It's at the local lab at the moment, being worked over by a data forensic team. I'm trying to get my hands on it."

He didn't have another computer. He glanced at Bailey, who was scrubbing a pot clean, managing to make even those small, repetitive motions sensual. God help him. "I better go."

"Stay out of trouble. Check in when you can."

He closed his phone and slipped it into his pocket, leaning back on the futon to watch her for a while. Her efficient movements, her focus on the task, her energy—he was trying to dissociate his thoughts from his baser instincts.

Linked to domestic terrorism.

He couldn't see it. Nobody could do a cover this good. If Bailey Preston had fooled him this thoroughly, he needed to retire from the business, he thought before he realized that he already had. Retired. He'd spent the past couple of months hating how that word tasted in his mouth. He hadn't exactly been discarded—he left willingly. And with a purpose. He'd planned on going back to Jakarta. And he didn't want the SDDU involved. He rubbed a hand over his chest, where a scar lay hidden under his shirt, and drew a full breath, appreciating that he could. He watched Bailey. Could she be in on all this? Was he losing his edge?

He stood and reached her in a few quiet steps. He went completely still for a moment before he grabbed her arm and twisted her, putting her into a restraining hold in a split second. He waited in vain for her reflex reaction.

The pot she'd been cleaning clanged to the floor.

She did nothing. Not a single defensive move. Didn't even try for his gun, which was still tucked in his waistband, even though he'd allowed her right hand to dangle dangerously close to it.

Instead, she twisted her head to look at him, with a thunderstorm gathering in her eyes. "What are you doing? Have you gone completely mad?"

As captivating as her eyes were, his gaze dropped to her mouth, just a few short inches from his. Perfectly pink and soft-looking.

"Let me go." She pushed against him exactly the wrong way when a simple lift-and-drop would have set her free. Clueless.

When he wouldn't budge, her lips flattened with fury. The need to taste her again—to drag his lips over hers, to feel her open, to invade and take—was overpowering. And because it was a *need,* and not some fleeting fancy or idle desire, he didn't allow himself to move one millimeter closer to her.

She froze and stared at him, drawing air in a little faster. Her pulse beat at the hollow of her throat. Had she guessed how badly he wanted to kiss her? That was all he needed. God only knew what she would make of that.

He let her go. When he was done with this—with her—he was going to take himself out for some serious R & R. "You need some self-defense lessons."

"No, thanks." She went for the pot.

He took another step back, removing himself from swinging distance, just in case. But she took the pot to the sink, rinsed it and filled it up.

Did her hand tremble for a moment? His were twitching as he fought against the need to reach for her again.

"Have you been working on anything interesting lately? On your computer?"

She flashed him a what-does-that-have-to-do-with-anything look. "Updated my Web site. Put up pictures of my latest sunflower twirlies."

He congratulated himself for not groaning aloud and rolling his eyes. Her garden-art side business drove him crazy. When she wasn't at work at the local garden center, she was in the garage, sawing and drilling and clanging and banging at all hours of the day and night. He hated the noise, knowing he wouldn't hear a damn thing if any of his old enemies were moving in to take him down.

Then there were her garden flags, on various sized poles, deftly placed to block sight of the road from his windows. If she'd flown the American flag on a regulation pole, he would have been fine with that. But her flags had daises on them, and sayings like It's Gardening Thyme.

He had to run one over so he would have a clear view of the road from his living room at least. She hadn't been happy. He'd been trying to build himself a defendable position, but she seemed determined to render him deaf and blind.

"Anything else?" he asked.

She shook her head. "Zak accidentally deleted a couple of my programs when he was here. I've been meaning to call someone to fix it."

Odd that she wouldn't ask him, since as far as she knew, he was a computer programmer. Or maybe not so odd, given their history.

"Did Zak use your computer a lot?"

"Only twenty-four seven." She gave a rueful smile. "He's a good kid. He's going through a tough time."

"What can be so tough at sixteen?"

She hesitated, drew a deep breath and shrugged. "His mother recently left. He's had some clashes with his dad. That's my brother."

That had to be hard on the kid. Cade thought back to the sullen looks the teenager had given him every time they'd run into each other outside. Had he resented being shipped off to his aunt? Could be he'd felt like his parents had got him out of the way while they were making decisions about their family's future. Without him.

Cade had been shuttled around between various relatives in his younger days, his mother always dealing with one emotional crisis or another. He could sympathize.

He looked at her. Her arms were wrapped around her waist as she stared off into space.

"You're worried about him." From what he'd been able to see, she'd taken good care of the kid while he'd been with her.

She looked up, chewing her lip for a second before speaking. "You know that plane that went down en route to Madrid a few weeks ago?"

He nodded.

"I could barely get him out of his room after that. I think it really freaked him out."

The crash and the FAA investigation that followed had been top news for the first part of the month. "Was anyone he knew on it?"

She shook her head and looked away. "My brother lives in Lower Manhattan." Her gaze returned to his. She blew some air out, and it ruffled the hair on her forehead. "When the twin towers went down, Zak was there," she said, with visible reluctance, her eyes dark. "He saw people jump, saw the bodies, saw the buildings collapse." She shook her head. "He was nine."

"Pachaimani." The name left his lips before he could stop himself.

"What?"

He drew a slow breath. "A brave little kid I used to know. Far from here." So Zak, too, had been traumatized. What kind of species did this to their children? Bailey's words made him see the brooding teen in a different light—he wished he had known while the boy had been there. "There's nothing to tie the Madrid flight to a terrorist act."

"I know. But we were watching the news and the pictures came on of the plane burning. And it was like… I can't explain it. Like he went into some lockdown mode. He went to his room and barely came out after that. And then he went home early. He was supposed to spend the whole summer with me." Her voice was barely audible over the rain as it drummed on the roof.

He'd been happy about Zak's going. The kid had hacked into his wireless system and tried to snoop around his files. But he hadn't gotten very far. Cade's laptop was beyond secure, his protection designed by Carly Tarasov, the SDDU's computer expert, the best of the best.

Which meant it wasn't likely that the FBI could trace anything back to it. Whatever they traced to the house had probably come from Bailey's PC. He couldn't picture Zak involved in domestic terrorism any more than he could picture Bailey, although there was no limit to the trouble a smart kid with nothing to do could get into just through sheer dumb luck. He could vouch for that.

But whatever the information was could have come from outside the house just as easily as from within. There were ways to remotely hijack someone's system. And there were ways to trace such an intrusion back to the source. Definitely worth a look.

"Want me to help with the food?" he asked her, noting the dejected slope of her shoulders. He liked her better when she had that storm brewing in her eyes, even if the thunderbolts were aimed at him.

"No," she said too quickly.

Scared her, had he? Everything he'd done so far, he'd done to keep them safe and free. But if she was scared of him, that was good. Really, just fine. It meant she would keep her distance, which was excellent, because he wasn't sure he could keep his. Their situation was already messed up beyond all repair. They didn't need any further complications.

He glanced at the futon and then away from it. Definitely not.

He walked to the window and scanned the lane and the rows of fishing cabins. The rain was still blowing around outside, the weather showing no sign of abating. "We'll eat, rest some, and then go take care of business."

"What business?" Her eyes narrowed with suspicion as she looked back at him from the hot plate.

She hadn't lied. She really did not trust him. Smart woman.

Smart and gorgeous. Tough, too. She'd handled the day pretty well so far. He resented the grudging admiration that was taking hold of him. He couldn't start liking her now. Lusting after her was bad enough. He was a professional. He needed to find that professional distance—fast.

"I have a bad feeling about whatever plan you're hatching." She dumped some dry noodles into the boiling water. "We could just lay low until the authorities figure out what's really going on. I don't think we should go out and do our own investigation.

Don't you think that's too dangerous? Let's just appreciate that we survived the day so far."

The very voice of reason. He bit back a smile. "I'm not a wait-and-see type of person."

She rolled her blue-violet eyes. "No. Really? I hadn't noticed." Her voice dripped with sarcasm.

The moment to disclose some further information had arrived. He needed to tell her his plan and get her on board because he couldn't leave her here. She might take off and get herself into more trouble than she could handle or worse—the people who were after them could catch up with her while he was gone.

"I need a partner." Maybe getting her involved in the mission would help her work up some enthusiasm for it.

"Partner in crime," she mumbled.

"Things would probably go easier and faster if we worked together."

She held up a hand, palm out, as if to separate herself from him. "We are not a team. I did not steal any cars. I take no responsibility for whatever felony you're plotting next."

"Glad I have your full confidence."

"Confidence has to be earned." She glared. "You jumped off a balcony with me!"

"Did you get hurt?"

She pressed her lips together. "You took me out on the lake in the middle of a storm, knowing I can't swim. Without a life preserver."

"Did you drown?"

"Do other people often fall for this the-end-justi-fies-the-means bullshit of yours?"

"First, the end rarely justifies the means. Second, when it does, I sure as hell don't stop to ask permission." Part of his job was to make judgment calls. Sometimes he had to choose between a terrible option and outright tragedy.

She waited a full minute, searching his face before she spoke again, her tone a tad more reasonable this time. "If it gets us out of this insanity—" she weighed her words "—maybe. Reluctant partners." She drew a deep breath that pressed her breasts against her shirt in a way that was most distracting. "So what's your latest brilliant idea?"

He resented the tone of her voice. But he didn't have time to worry about what she thought of him. It was bad enough that on some level he actually cared. *Don't go there.*

Okay, Bailey, here it comes.

"We are going to borrow another car, then break into the FBI's local office," he said as fast as he could, hoping she might miss the stickiest parts of the sentence.

Judging by the way her eyes widened and her jaw dropped, she hadn't missed a thing.

Chapter Five

Bailey leaned forward and let the man behind the desk catch a better glimpse of her cleavage. Cade stifled a groan, pretending deep interest in the settings on his camera. They were the only two visitors in the sparse waiting area at the FBI's Newtown Square office, the hum of the air conditioner providing the background music for the not-so-subtle seduction that was happening at the front desk.

"It's so nice in here. The weather is stifling outside. Too much humidity from that rain." She fanned herself, pushing her breasts even farther out.

If the guy wasn't careful, he was going to lose an eye. But the man seemed oblivious to danger.

"I'm just parched." She licked her lips. Leisurely.

Cade shifted in his seat. Only because he was missing the feel of his gun at his back. He wasn't one of those guys who felt off-kilter and naked without a weapon, but given a choice, he'd just as soon have it in his waistband, against his skin.

"Can I get you something to drink? We have a break

room in the back." The man looked like he would have been willing to offer a kidney if she needed it.

"You're so sweet. I'm fine, thank you. But do you think I might use the little girls' room?" She flashed a coy smile.

He pushed a button and motioned her through the second checkpoint, which was unmanned at the moment. They'd already passed through the metal detectors just inside the front entrance. "First door to the right."

Cade set aside the camera he had picked up at a local shop to round out their cover. He tapped his foot on the industrial gray carpet, hoping the information they had on the layout of the building was correct, hoping that Bailey could perform her task without running into any trouble.

They could have waited until nightfall and maybe had an easier time getting in. Maybe. He was pretty good at doctoring locks and security systems, but without better tools and sufficient research, he'd determined the risks were too great. And he hadn't wanted to wait. So they'd shown up as Jane Weigel, reporter from the *Philadelphia Inquirer,* and her photographer. They had an appointment with Agent Rubliczky about a new development in one of his old cases, they'd said.

Rubliczky was out because Cade had asked the Colonel to call the agent away for a meeting. He had prepped Bailey for her part of the mission and damn if she wasn't a natural—she played the flirty reporter to perfection. The receptionist bought it down to the last tantalizing glimpse of her pale-blue lace bra. Hell, Cade was still hot and bothered from watching her seduce him.

The guy at the front desk was looking down the hallway after Bailey with rapture in his eyes, not wanting to miss a moment of her reappearance. Pitiful. Only two minutes passed. Cade settled in to wait with a bored expression on his face.

He didn't have to wait for her too long.

She smiled at the receptionist as she sashayed by him on the way back, then sat next to Cade. "I think we'll start with a quick summary of the case. Play up the age angle." She sounded professional and preoccupied.

Five, four, three, two, one. The fire alarm went off on cue.

The receptionist stood as he was shutting down his computer. "I'm sorry. We'll have to evacuate. Emergency procedures."

"No problem." Cade strode to the door, showing only the slightest annoyance, and opened it for Bailey as people were filing out from the back offices. He watched them in the glass without turning around taking a head count. "We'll wait in the car."

They did, until it looked like everyone had come out. Four men and one woman—the ones who had the bad luck to be on weekend duty and a few who had hot cases running, he figured.

"Good job in there." He kept his eyes on them as he talked to Bailey.

"I thought I was going to pass out from nerves," she said.

But when he turned to her, he found her grinning. He knew why. He never felt as alive as during an op. And even if this one was pretty tame compared to most he'd been involved in, it was her first. And, let's hope to God, her last. If the Colonel knew he was involving a civilian in this, he would have Cade's head. Cade turned back to the FBI office.

"Do you really have to go back in?"

"Only if we want to figure out what's going on. We are in trouble. I want to know how deep and how to get out of it. I need to see what they have on us." He glanced at her.

She wasn't smiling anymore. "Take your gun?" She popped the glove compartment open.

He hesitated for a second. He couldn't really shoot an FBI agent. If things came to that— They wouldn't. "It stays. If…"

Her eyes were dark with worry. "Yes?"

He decided not to say what he'd been about to say. "If lover boy comes to find you, just tell him I've gone off to stretch my legs. Keep him busy." He offered a teasing grin.

She remained serious. "Be careful."

"You bet."

He slipped from the car and circled around the building at a distance and didn't stop until he was in line with the bathroom window Bailey had left open for him. Good girl.

Nobody back here. Nothing but bushes. He made his

way to the wall undetected, pulling on rubber gloves he'd picked up at the pharmacy on their way here.

He stopped to stare.

Close up, the opening proved to be smaller than it had appeared from afar when they'd circled the building during their twenty-minute recon. It had a wide outer frame, which he hadn't fully seen from the bushes. The part of the window that actually opened was—

He consciously shifted his thoughts from focusing on the problem to moving forward, toward a solution. He wasn't the type to walk away without trying.

He spent many long minutes attempting to get his shoulders through, performing moves that would have given a world-class extortionist a run for his money. At least he didn't have to worry about making too much noise with the fire alarm still going.

A minuscule adjustment in angle allowed him to push through at last, and he glanced up at the motion detector in the corner above the double sink. The indicator light was off. Since even the smaller, regional FBI offices like this had some weekend coverage, the security system wasn't on. No security cameras in the bathroom, either. Three hoorays for employee privacy.

He did have to make sure to keep his head down, however, when he stepped out to the hallway. He'd be recorded, but one of the rules of the game was not to worry about stuff that couldn't be helped. They would know someone had been in here once they found Bailey's hard drive gone, anyway. He tried to keep his face covered as best as he could and hoped they wouldn't be able to identify him. The FBI security cameras weren't like the ones at the corner convenience stores. No grainy, gray images here, no blurring. The video would have such high resolution they could count the small hairs on a fly's behind.

He went straight to the computer lab. The Colonel had connections and had been able to tell him the exact location. All he was missing was an ID card for the scanner but it wasn't a problem. When the emergency system was on, the scanner could be disabled by using an emergency override code on the keypad next to it. He had the code, thanks to the Colonel, who was risking his entire career and the future of the SDDU for him. The unconditional vote of confidence was humbling.

He was in the room a second later and going through the carefully labeled bags of evidence. Bailey's hard drive was close to the top, identified by case number, date and address. It had come in only a couple of hours before, according to the date stamp. And had obviously already been worked on.

He stuck the piece of damning electronics under his shirt and was about to hightail it out of there when the alarm stopped. And after the ringing cleared in his ears, he could hear people talking. And coming closer.

Damn. He threw himself onto his stomach behind a desk and hoped that anyone walking by wouldn't see him through the window in the door. Who the hell were they? Firemen? Security? Wouldn't security also leave the building in a fire? Or would they check first to make sure there *was* a fire? He didn't know what the FBI protocol was for the given situation since his job had never been about spending time in an office. He hated when he didn't have time to prep for an op. Working with incomplete intel was a good way to get your head shot off.

He stayed put and listened, swearing when he couldn't make out a word through the security glass. He glanced through a crack between two tables. Not firemen. They had no protective gear. The two men wore white shirts with ties.

He couldn't get caught. Bailey was waiting for him in the car. He hoped that if he didn't come out, she'd just get behind the steering wheel and drive away. He should have given her "in case of emergency" instructions, but she'd looked all stressed out that he was going back into the building.

Cade kept his attention on the men through the crack. *Okay, boys, time to move on.* He had to get out before fire rescue got here. They would check every room carefully to determine what had set off the alarm. He'd have to take the homemade smoke bomb from the ladies' room with him when he left.

A tense moment passed before the men finally stopped yakking and walked away. Right in the direction he was supposed to be going. Damn.

He ran through the building's blueprint in his head. Not much else he could use in the way of an escape route. The office windows were the kind that didn't open, unlike in the bathroom. Trying to make it up to another floor didn't make any sense. There was no fire-escape staircase—he had checked that during recon. That left the roof, but with the building being five stories high, jumping was out of the question. Even if the roof were lower, he couldn't have jumped. He would have made too much noise in the bushes in the back, and in the front he would have been seen by the office staff milling around the building, waiting for the all clear so they could go back in. And he would bet his currently inaccessible bank account that most of them were armed.

The downstairs bathrooms were his only chance. He kept low and made it to the door, looking out. The hallway was empty. He eased outside and moved at a fast clip along the wall. The time to hesitate was over. Oh, hell, there never *had* been time to hesitate. If he bumped into anyone, he would punch their lights out and run like crazy.

But he made it back to the ladies' room without trouble and breathed a sigh of relief before grabbing the remains of the smoke bomb and squeezing out the window. He was slipping back into the nondescript Oldsmobile he'd "acquired" despite Bailey's squealing protest when the first fire truck turned the corner, sirens blaring full force.

"Anything happen out here?" He watched fire rescue arriving as he turned the key in the ignition.

"I sat tight like you told me. And sent positive thoughts to the universe. Find anything?" She was holding her breath, her hands clasped tight in her lap, her fine body vibrating with nerves.

He pulled away from the curb. Frankly, the question rankled. When he engaged in an operation, he saw to it that it was done. "What do you think?" He patted his shirt. *Ye of little faith.*

"What's that?"

"Encoded stuff. I'm going to need a friend to read it for me."

She relaxed back against her seat. "I thought for sure that we would get caught."

Deep breath in, deep breath out. Her breasts were moving against her top in a most interesting way. Not that he noticed.

"It almost seemed…too easy." She blew air through pursed lips.

"There's much to be said for simple plans." He turned onto the main road, but not in the direction of the little shack that waited for them across the Maryland border. "They have good security, but not Pentagon good. It's the FBI and just a small field office at that. The bad guys are usually running from them, not toward them. I don't think they get a lot of burglary attempts."

He drove to the nearest McDonald's, parked and made a call. He didn't identify himself. The person on the other end would know who he was by his ID code on the display.

"Would you look over a hard drive for me?" he asked without preamble. He hadn't set this up ahead of time, because he didn't want to give anyone time to track any calls and head him off. But Carly Tarasov was okay with having things sprung on her. She was born for this business: sharp, tough and flexible.

"How is retirement treating you?" she asked, with a smile in her voice.

"It's not as quiet as I'd hoped." He might have exaggerated the rueful tone a tad.

Carly, the SDDU's top computer expert, laughed on the other end of the line. "You'd hate quiet."

She was right. "How is the baby?"

"More trouble than a double mission."

He believed that. His sister had two-year-old twin boys. He'd seen prison camps in Southeast Asia that were less scary than being left alone in a room with those two.

"Can you bring it over?" she asked.

"I'd prefer a drop-off."

There was a moment of silence on the other end. Cade knew she was realizing that he was in the middle of something serious, not a routine job. "Where?"

He gave his location.

"I'll be over in twenty minutes. Try not to get into any trouble before I get there."

"You know me."

"That's why I worry. You need backup on this? I've been itching to get out of the house."

He smiled at her wistful tone, then glanced at Bailey. "I got it. Thanks."

And before Carly could try to talk him into giving her a break from changing diapers, her husband, Nick—another member of their unit—came on the line. "Are you getting my wife involved in anything I'm going to have to make you regret later?"

"I'm regretting it already." And that was the truth.

Domestic terrorism was not a charge to be taken lightly. And it wasn't just the FBI looking for him— there had been the tangos with that grenade launcher. "Heard anything through the grapevine about any tangos coming stateside?" he asked, knowing that the chances for a positive answer were slim. The members of the SDDU worked alone for the most part. Nick would know only the details of whatever he was personally involved in. Even the Colonel, who had an overview of everything, hadn't been able to come up with any usable information yet.

"No, but I'll keep an ear out. Need backup?"

"Not yet. I'll let you know." He would have hated to involve the Tarasovs any more than he already had.

"You do that. And make sure nothing happens to my girl." Tarasov was as cool an operator as Cade had ever seen, but when it came to his wife, he had a tendency to go crazy even over the smallest thing.

"You bet."

He hung up and wrapped the hard drive in a sweat-shirt he'd brought with him, picking the most optimally placed table outside where he could accidentally leave it once Carly showed.

BAILEY STARED AT THE ROAD ahead of them, her mind reeling. What she had just seen Cade do, she had only seen in spy movies before. If she had known who her new neighbor was when he'd moved in, she would have probably run screaming for the hills. Not that she knew much now. Except that he definitely wasn't a computer programmer. And that he wasn't going to tell her the full truth anytime soon. Probably not ever.

"You're too quiet." He shot her a questioning look. His caramel eyes looked dark chocolate now that the sun had gone down.

"Just thinking that until now, I could honestly say that whatever they thought they had against me, I was innocent. Now that I've broken into the FBI…" God, it didn't bear thinking about.

Several counts of grand theft auto, plus breaking and entering into a government facility. And she had a feeling they weren't done yet. Was this what they called "the point of no return" in the movies? There was definitely no going back from here, no going to the cops. She had to ride it out with Cade and see if his plan worked. If it didn't… She closed her eyes and fought back the panic.

"You didn't break in anywhere. You went to the bathroom and opened a window to air the place out. That's not a crime."

"If you think they'll—"

"If this goes down badly, I kidnapped you. Got that?"

Self-sacrifice? She really didn't know the man at all. The guy who'd annoyed her from morning to night for the past three months wouldn't do something like this. "Let's just make sure nothing goes wrong."

"I'm working on it," he said.

By the time they got back to the cabin, it was nearly eleven—he'd taken several detours to make sure that nobody followed them.

He pulled the car into the lean-to and tossed a tarp over it. "We'll get rid of it tomorrow."

Thank God for that. She didn't have it in her to leave the car somewhere down the road and then walk back a few more miles tonight.

He went in first, not letting her follow until he thoroughly inspected the place. And she couldn't resent him for that. She was aware that without him, she'd be sitting on a metal chair in a sparse room with a grumpy FBI agent yelling questions at her from behind a bright light—or worse.

Instead, she was still free, comfortably full—they'd eaten a couple of hamburgers while they'd waited for Cade's "friend," who turned out to be a gorgeous blonde—and about to get some rest after a day straight from hell.

She kicked off her shoes, walked to the bathroom and picked up the plastic bowl, holding it out to Cade. "So who's going to take a bath first?" She couldn't help the sarcasm.

He took the bowl and set it aside. "I think we'd be more comfortable in the lake."

Having her whole body immersed in cool water sounded like heaven. But she was wary of the lake at night. "How deep is the water?"

"There's a shallow beach a little way down from the docks."

"I don't have a bathing suit."

"Neither do I."

Her pulse sped up. Skinny-dipping with Cade Palmer. Interesting. And probably to be avoided at all costs.

He opened his mouth, and she expected him to say something suggestive.

"We'll be fine in our T-shirts," he said.

Full of surprises, this man.

"Okay," she agreed against her better judgment. Maybe bathing in the lake was the right thing to do. It would certainly take longer than a sponge bath, with the walk down there and back. It should give her some extra time to strategize about how she was going to handle the futon situation.

But strategizing could not have been further from her mind fifteen minutes later, as she stood waist deep in the water and watched Cade break the surface a few feet away. He didn't wear his T-shirt, leaving everything on the beach except his midnight-blue boxers. She'd already inched her way into the water by then, too late to retreat.

With the water glistening on his wide, muscular shoulders and running down his chest in rivulets, he looked like—

"Isn't this nice?" he asked.

"Mmm." She didn't trust her voice.

"This should cool us off enough to get a good night's sleep."

She hadn't yet felt a cooling effect but was ready for it. Any minute now. Please.

She stepped back, hoping to put some distance between them, and stumbled into a hole in the muddy lake bottom, losing her footing and slipping under. He was there in a split second, hauling her up. Against his hard body.

There really was only so much temptation a woman could take. She allowed herself to rest against him for a second. His arm was around her waist. Her face tilted to his.

"Are you okay?" His voice was an octave lower than usual.

The moment was spoiled only by her wet hair plastered down on her face. She probably looked like a drowned rat.

"Fine." She blinked water from her eyes and brushed her hair behind her ears.

Still, he didn't let her go.

"We should probably go in." She needed to get away from him before the desire to feel his lips on hers won and she made a fool of herself. "Someone might see us."

"They'll think we're lovers, messing around in the night." He lowered his head an inch.

Her mouth went dry.

"It wouldn't hurt to work on that cover a little." His breath fanned her face. Then slowly, deliberately, his mouth opened over hers.

Her hands slipped to his waist so she could steady herself, then moved onto the muscles of his back. Her spine tingled with pleasure as he slowly tasted her, taking his time, brushing his mouth against hers, applying a little pressure.

She knew what he wanted. And she seemed powerless to deny him. She opened for him and drowned in the sensation of her tongue meeting his. And after another second, she realized that she was in so much trouble here.

If there was a guy in this universe who was absolutely, utterly, irrevocably the wrong man for her, it was the one whose tongue was doing the slow waltz with hers. For one, she still had no idea who he really was, other than a dangerous man.

But her body didn't care. All it wanted was more, more, more. They must have been on the same wavelength because he tilted her in his arms, slanted his mouth over hers for better access and systematically liquefied her bones.

HE HAD TO STOP. AS IN now. As in five minutes ago. If he didn't, he was going to take her right here in the water.

Her mouth was sweet and hot. Her body fit perfectly against his. Okay, so he had lusted after her pretty much since he'd moved in. So maybe he'd played up how annoying she was to make sure he kept his distance, and was annoying back to make sure she kept hers. He'd been clear all along that something like this was a bad idea. So why couldn't he remember that now?

Okay, he remembered it. Dimly. But for the life of him, he couldn't act on the quiet voice of sanity that whispered "Don't go there" from the distance.

Her breasts slid into his palms. It had to have happened that way, because he sure as hell didn't remember going for them. But there they were, filling his hands, their firm weight nearly bringing him to his knees.

"Bailey?"

He couldn't be asking what he thought he was asking.

"I think we should go back," he said quickly before she could answer. For good measure, he let go of her and stepped away.

"Uh-huh."

"You go on. I'll stay a little longer." Long enough for the cold water to flatten the front of his boxer shorts.

"Okay." She turned and took a reluctant step away from him.

"I'm sorry."

"Hey, no big deal. Just for our cover, right?" She wouldn't look at him.

Not right. In fact, she couldn't have been more wrong. But it would have been the flat-out stupidest thing to tell her. "Sure."

She took the second step faster, then the third. And he stood there, staring after her like a jackass as she gracefully walked from the water and across the beach, her long T-shirt plastered to that incredible body, which wasn't going to allow his imagination a moment of rest tonight.

When she disappeared into the shack and the lights came on in the window, he turned and threw himself into the water. A good swim was what he needed. He planned on being bone tired before he went back there.

SHE WAS ALONE IN THE shack. Cade was alone in the lake. Well, he didn't fancy swimming. He stayed by the window instead and watched the woman slip out of her wet T-shirt and underwear. Cade would come out of that water sooner or later and come to her.

He'd lost them on the way to Maryland, but the man he occasionally blackmailed at the FBI had let him know as soon as they had new information, which had brought him to the train station next to the lake. After that it had been a matter of going through the small community of fishing cabins one by one until he'd found what he was looking for.

At exactly the right time. Luck again. He smiled as he watched.

She had full breasts, tipped with rose-colored, large nipples like exotic berries. A slim waist, flat stomach. She wasn't overly thin like the always-starving whores of Jakarta, with their sharp hip bones and their ribs showing too much as they bent over him. There was a supple softness to this one that he liked.

He was moving toward the door when he sensed an approaching presence. Not Cade. He couldn't have gotten out of the water this fast.

He pulled back into the shadows again and slinked away from the shack. Impatience never got anyone anywhere but the grave.

GOING MORE THAN HALFWAY across the lake and back did the trick. Cade had swum miles and miles in rehab to strengthen his lungs after they'd taken the shrapnel from his chest. He'd used the monotonous exercise back then to numb his mind, just as he was using it now to numb his body.

The beach was no longer deserted when he got back.

A small bonfire burned on shore. Three college girls were skinny-dipping, the water just below their naked breasts.

"Excuse me, ladies. Coming out," he said, giving warning.

Instead of ducking into the water, they giggled.

If they didn't care, he sure as hell didn't. He looked away from them and headed for shore.

"Are you staying here?" one of them called after him when he was in the waist-high shallows.

"Leaving in the morning."

"How come we didn't see you?"

"I'm usually early to bed."

"Want to come for a swim with us?" Her friends giggled again.

The invitation was clear. And at any other time in his life, he would have taken it. He had been thinking not that long ago about a little R & R very much like this to get Bailey out from under his skin. But now he couldn't get away from the girls fast enough.

"I think I'll be turning in. But thanks." He waded out of the water and gathered up his T-shirt.

"You can warm up by our fire." The words dripped innuendo.

Cade didn't like fire. He'd even blocked the fireplace at the new house, pushing a dresser in front of it. He hated looking at anything that was sooty black, hated the smell of smoke in his nose.

He kept on walking.

"If you change your mind, we'll be here."

He headed toward the shack without responding to them.

He needed all right—wanted—but not what those girls were offering. He wanted Bailey, a disconcerting thought. He loved the fairer sex and took any presented opportunity to enjoy them, not that his job had left him with a lot of time to fool around during the past twenty years.

Women. Not a specific one. Not ever.

If the blonde at the bar insisted on taking him home, fine. But if he ended up with her brunette friend instead, he wasn't too put out. He had never wanted one specific woman the way he wanted Bailey. Bailey Preston and nobody else.

Damn.

He could have her. Long night. One bed.

She had responded to him back in the water. The memory of that was enough to get him hard all over again. He'd just have to live with it. No way was he going for another swim. Not with the collegiate barracudas out there. But Bailey...

He could see her through the window as she was getting ready for bed. Maybe he could have her. Then again, she had proved herself to be pretty sensible so far. Maybe he couldn't. That thought bothered him more than it should have.

Suddenly his senses sounded the high alarm, and the next second he had picked out the shadow behind the empty shack next door, less than twenty feet from him. But knowing someone was there meant nothing. He had no weapon. No cover.

The metal of a gun flashed in the moonlight as the man took a step forward and said, "Put your hands above your head and drop to your knees."

Chapter Six

Cade took a moment to assess his options. The guy was so close, he had a sure shot. Damn. He should have taken his gun to the beach. Except that he couldn't have taken it into the water and he wouldn't leave a loaded gun on shore, where anyone could come across it. Which left him unarmed. Again.

His three months of retirement must have slow cooked his brain. Or maybe Bailey Preston had done that.

He glanced toward the lean-to from the corner of his eye, without moving his head. If he could grab one of the paddles, maybe he could draw the attacker away from the shack—away from Bailey— and fast. Before she decided to look out and see why he wasn't back yet. She had the tendency to be as much trouble as humanly possible in any given situation.

He shifted his weight slightly, getting ready to lunge. "I wouldn't try it," the man said. Damn his eyes.

He shouldn't have seen such a slight movement in the dark. "To your knees, buddy."

That cocky drawl was familiar. "Joey?" Cade asked.

Joey Tanner stayed motionless for another second before stepping forward into the light filtering from the window, his face finally revealed. "Cade? What in hell are you doing here?" He lowered his gun.

"Last I heard you were out of the country, or I would have called." The kid had caught him without a gun. What in the hell was wrong with him? He'd been slacking off for weeks now, trying to act like a normal person and not a killing machine. Was he changing for Bailey? Hell of a time to realize it. He shook out the T-shirt in his left hand and pulled it over his head. What had he expected would come from all of this, anyway?

"Got back last night." Joey put the safety on his gun. "You're always welcome at the Bass Palace." He looked Cade over, measuring him up. "Heard you retired."

"Decided to dedicate my life to the ladies." He didn't want to get into his last mission, especially not his injuries, or why he had taken retirement when it had been offered to him, instead of fighting tooth and nail to stay on the team.

Joey read his tone and posture right, and didn't push. "Wishful thinking, eh? That's always good. Gotta keep positive."

Cade didn't miss the angry welt above Joey's left eye. Had to be a story behind that row of stitches. A story he wanted badly to hear—he did miss the action. But they wouldn't be swapping war tales. Security clearance within the SDDU did not extend beyond one's own missions. If he asked straight-out, Joey would claim a car accident with enough conviction that he'd probably believe him.

"Got back last night and your first trip was to the lake?" Cade could hear the "I'm not buying that" tone in his own voice. "How did you know someone was here?"

"You tripped the silent alarm. There are weight sensors in the floor. As soon as someone steps inside, it rings my cell." Joey was grinning from ear to ear.

Cade grinned back. Joey had always been a sucker for technology. "That's new. Gadget Man?"

Joey's smile faded. "Yeah."

Gadget Man was a guy on the unit who was a marvel with technology. He had set them up with tailor-made tools for special missions—there were few in the SDDU who could say they didn't owe their lives to him. But Gadget Man had gone missing almost a year ago somewhere in sub-Saharan Africa and not even all the intelligence at the Colonel's fingertips could find him.

"So who's the babe in there?" Joey asked after a short pause. "I wouldn't mind getting to know her. Unless, you know, you're—"

"We're not."

Joey was grinning again. "Funny that. Your mouth says *no,* but your eyes say *mine.*"

"You can't even see my face in the dark." Cade hated the snap in his voice as well as the all-knowing glint in Joey's eyes.

"Let's get inside then, where there's light and a hot babe to be had."

Joey the Kid. Cade shook his head. At twenty-seven, Joey Tanner was one of the youngest men in the SDDU. He was utterly and unashamedly obsessed with big guns, fast cars and easy women.

He could warn Joey about just where Bailey rated on the easy scale. But it'd be much more fun to watch him find out.

"After you," Cade said, noticing that while they'd been talking, the light inside had gone out. Had Bailey gone to bed without waiting up for him? He had sort of hoped they'd be going to bed together. As in the two of them. Minus Joey Tanner.

Joey tucked his gun into his waistband and covered it with his shirt before opening the door. He was reaching for the light switch when Cade saw his own handgun move in from the right and connect with Joey's temple.

"Stay right where you are." To her credit, Bailey managed to say the words like she meant them.

And damn if that hard resolution in her voice didn't shoot a flash of heat to his groin. Hot.

"All right, honey, easy now." Joey's voice carried a dose of surprise and a hint of turn-on, too. Which irritated the hell out of Cade. "It's just us. That ugly wart, Cade, and Joey Tanner, his good-looking friend."

"Cade?" she called out, sounding uncertain now.

"I'm right behind him. Everything's all right. He owns this place."

She took her sweet time before she lowered the gun.

Joey flicked on the light and turned a million-watt smile on her. "I prefer to call it my Bass Palace."

She looked wide-eyed and flushed, her breath coming fast and her chest rising with it. No smile lit up her face. She'd been scared. But before he could react to that thought, Cade realized that she had changed her clothes. He had a hard time taking his eyes off her white tank top and the pink shorts which hugged her in interesting ways.

Joey hadn't missed any of that, either, judging from the appreciative look on his freshly patched-up face. Which could easily come to meet with another bruise or two before the night was out.

"Down, boy," Cade said under his breath.

"I'm sorry. I didn't know what was going on out there. Come in." Bailey stepped away, still holding the gun.

Cade scowled. There were two guns in play, and he had nothing. Not counting the repeat action in his pants, which he hoped to hell the other two couldn't see. Hot damn, but she was sexy when she took charge of a situation like that. Who knew? Okay, he did. He'd seen her go at a four-by-four with a band saw in her garage once. She ruled lumber—yes, ma'am. In a flowery fairy skirt and halter top, accessorized with steel-toed boots, protective gloves and safety goggles holding back that tumble of cinnamon hair. He nearly drove right through his own garage door while staring at her.

"Thank you, darlin'." Joey followed her in, casting a glance at Cade. "My kind of woman," he said so only Cade would hear.

JOEY TANNER STAYED FOR an hour or so and flirted shamelessly the whole time. He wasn't serious— Bailey was pretty sure about that—but she appreciated his taking her mind off the severity of their situation. That, and he provided a nice buffer for the thickening sexual tension that had started between Cade and her in the water. She'd been jumping out of her skin with anticipation, waiting for him to come back. And her nerves had frayed even more when she'd heard the voice of a stranger outside.

She flashed Joey a smile over the white plastic table. Saved by the bell.

He was originally from Louisiana, which was why he had to have a little something near water now that he lived in the Northeast. He talked about crawfish, bayous and alligator wrestling.

He was young, bursting with energy and impossibly handsome. That open smile of his never left his face. He was a contrast to Cade, who was becoming more and more morose as the night wore on.

"Better get going." Joey stood at last, well after midnight. "Stay as long as you like," he said to Cade, then looked at her on his way out the door. "You're welcome to anything I have."

Cade suddenly had a coughing fit, and Joey's

smile widened. "Good luck. I'll be stateside for the next—" he glanced at his watch "—four hours. Call me if there's anything I can do to help."

YOU'VE DONE MORE THAN enough, Cade thought. He stood to walk Joey outside. When they were through the door, he decided not to give the guy a matching split above the other eye as he'd been tempted to do for the past hour or so. He inhaled the cool night air. "Let me know if you hear anything. Going anywhere near my old hunting grounds?" he asked, not expecting much of an answer.

"Private mission." The smile slid off Joey's face for the first time.

Interesting. "Colonel knows about that?"

"Can't put the team in jeopardy. If the mission goes down badly, he can say I went rogue." Joey shrugged. "I have some off time. I'm using that."

Cade understood. This was exactly why he had taken retirement. His final hunt wasn't going to be pretty. Whatever he had to do to get his man, he would. And he didn't want anyone else to catch flack for that. "Going after an old enemy?"

"Going after the woman I love." Joey's smile crept back.

Cade smirked. So Joey had been just busting his chops all night about Bailey. Good to know—for Joey's sake. "That serious, huh?"

"Serious as a Daisy Cutter."

The BLU-82B/C-130 weapon system, nick-named Commando Vault in Vietnam and then Daisy

Cutter during the Afghan war, was the largest conventional bomb the military had. As serious as business could get, with a nine-hundred-foot lethal radius. "She in trouble?"

"Stuck in a Darfur refugee camp near the Sudanese border. She's an aid worker."

"I thought they weren't letting foreign aid workers into those camps anymore." Violence was rising in the region again.

"She's looking for the kids of a murdered friend." Cade could hear the worry in Joey's voice. "She got someone to fly her in, bribed the man in charge and was supposed to fly out the same day with the four kids. That was a week ago." His face went dark. "Haven't heard from her since."

"Could be they confiscated the plane and she had to find another way back." Cade said the only optimistic thing he could think of, knowing that the reality of the situation was possibly much grimmer.

"The Sub-Saharan Security Council is visiting the United Nations this week in New York, trying to come up with solutions. If they fail, if they don't get the UN resolution they came for…"

He could tell from Joey's voice that that was exactly what everyone in the know expected to happen.

"All hell is going to break loose." Joey drew a slow breath. "The talks will end tomorrow. I have to get there before that and get her out."

"You'll find her." Hell, if he weren't in the middle of his own mess, he'd go with him.

"You better believe it." Joey hesitated a moment. "She might be—"

"She's not. She's fine."

"Not that. I think she might be pregnant."

Wow. "Yeah?" He grinned at the kid, clapping him on the back. "Way to go."

"I don't know." Joey looked dazed by the possibility. "She kind of hinted the last time we talked over the phone. I think she wanted to tell me in person, when we were together again." He offered a tight smile. "Better get going. I'm flying out of Baltimore in a couple of hours. I'll call you if I hear anything."

"I'd appreciate that." Although chances were slim that Joey would happen upon relevant information for Cade's troubles while in the Sudan. He'd only been on two ops on that whole continent, both times in Nigeria.

Still, a small chance was better than no chance at all. And he desperately needed a break. "If you need me for anything, let me know. I'll find a way to help."

His cell phone rang just as he walked back inside. The display showed Carly's ID code. "What's up?"

"Am I on speaker?" was the first question she asked, which set off some alarm bells.

"No."

"Good. Want the bad news or the bad news?" She went on without waiting for his answer. "Your pretty little friend there is not who she seems to be. Tie her up and bring her in."

He glanced over at Bailey, who was looking at him curiously. That white tank top was going to be the death of him. Too tight, too thin, too everything. He could get into the tying-up thing. Definitely. But he didn't think Carly meant what he was fantasizing about. Nor did Bailey look like she was ready to get naughty with him. A shame. "Tell me what you know."

"I tracked communications to and from her PC. Wasn't easy. That one gave me a run for my money. When you bring her in, I definitely want to talk to her. Hacker. First-rate."

He stared at Bailey. She'd left him to his call and was now grabbing pillows for the futon, shaking out a blanket, all graceful innocence. And all he could think of was kissing her in the lake. He was harder than a billy goat in heat. *Look away. Focus on Carly.* "Are you sure?"

"It takes one to know one."

Right. Carly had been a first-class hacker and had even spent time at a federal resort for it before she'd been recruited to the SDDU by Nick, who later married her.

"She hacked into some terrorist circles."

That cooled him considerably. "What? When?" He felt stupider than shit all of a sudden. He'd been hoping Carly would find nothing but whimsical sunflower and bumblebee garden-flag designs. That was how far he was gone. *Come on back, boy. Return from the edge.*

"Six weeks ago is the first trail I can see," Carly went on.

Now he didn't dare look at Bailey, didn't want her to read something in his eyes. He wanted a moment to digest this before confronting her.

"The flight that went down? She claims she did

that. Electromagnetic pulse box. Highly effective. Undetectable."

"Impossible."

"Not hardly. In any case, word got out, and there's a bidding war over it."

His head was reeling. "Who?"

"All the big players in the illegal-weapons game. You name it. And the communications definitely originated on the PC that had the hard drive you dropped off. It's not a case of her accounts being hijacked remotely. She's the one."

He swore under his breath. The illegal-weapons market was getting out of hand. One man used to control it all, a guy named Tsernyakov. But since the SDDU took him down, the business had fragmented to a few of his top men, each player vying to replace him, doing his best to prove that he could be just as crazy, just as ruthless, just as violent. The situation was worse now than when Tsernyakov had been alive.

That would explain the tangos with the grenade launcher aiming at the garage instead of his bedroom. They weren't aiming for him. They were aiming for her—not to kill her, just to bring her outside. If he hadn't grabbed her first, she would probably be out of the country by now. And if she couldn't produce the weapon she had promised, she would be dead.

So none of this had to do with his old enemies. Or Abhi. He crossed that off his mental list. Which meant his hunt was still on, just as soon as he could get back to it. He had waited too long already.

Three months ago, he could barely wait to get out

of the hospital in Germany and go after Smith. He had moved into his uncle's place to recoup and at one point, his plans had lost some of their urgency, thanks to Bailey. There had been garden flags to push around and sparks flying and fights to be had. For a couple of weeks, he hadn't thought as much about Pachai-mani. He had made promises to that ten-year-old kid, promises he meant to keep.

He looked at Bailey. A fine distraction. And suspected domestic terrorist. Damn. He hadn't seen *that* coming.

He could call the Colonel and have her picked up. He was retired. She wasn't his problem to deal with. Within an hour, he could be back on track and meeting with Abhi. Except that every instinct he had said that something was off here.

And damn if he could see himself handing Bailey over to anyone. Not just yet.

"While I was looking around in cyberspace, I also might have accidentally opened some memos from your old pals," Carly said.

He grinned. Gotta love Carly. "Anything interesting?"

"They tracked your friend's communications back to your address, too. They'd asked for permission to put the house under surveillance and were going to start this week. There is a report on both of you. Cade, Cade, Cade," she tsked.

He wondered just how much the FBI knew about his preretirement activities. Nothing, if the Colonel had anything to do with it. And yet they must have known that he'd been in the SDDU, because they'd gone to ask the Colonel about him. Damn.

"So they knew the location of the communications, and they had you pegged for it."

Made sense if they'd compared his rap sheet with Bailey's. There was nothing remotely shady out there on her. He'd looked. Her record was pretty much her résumé. It was either genuine or the best cover-up job he'd ever seen.

"You need help bringing her in?" Carly asked.

"Give me some time to figure this out." He thanked her before hanging up.

"Anything new? Can we go home yet?" Bailey was shaking the dust out of something that looked more like roadkill than a pillow. She looked sexy. And innocent. The picture of domesticity.

She was not a weapons dealer, he was pretty sure about that. He'd checked her out thoroughly before moving in next door, for his own safety. He might have missed a thing or two, but he wouldn't have missed something like that.

And yet he'd been fooled before, and had the bullet hole in his left thigh to remind him. He walked to the table and said, "Let's sit down and have a little talk." He sank into his chair, and when she sat down opposite him with a puzzled expression on her face, he put his gun on the table between them.

SOMETHING BAD HAD happened. She could see it in the way he grew more focused, more calculated.

Bailey sat still. "Who was that on the phone? Is something wrong?"

"Gig is up. It's the end of the road. Is there anything you would like to tell me?" His words were carefully measured.

I find it sexy when you go all tough-guy, but at the same time, it scares me a little. Nope. Definitely not that. She pressed her lips tight and waited a beat. "Like what?"

"How about your little side business?"

"You hate my garden statuettes." He rarely missed a chance to mock them.

"Anything else you do on the side for extra cash?"

Something in his voice put her defenses up, and all of a sudden she was no longer distracted by his wide shoulders and broad chest. Any wayward image that might have floated into her mind while making up the futon was banished from her head. "Maybe this would be quicker if you just came right out and told me what you're accusing me of."

"Where did you learn your computer skills?"

She blinked. "What?"

But he didn't explain his odd question. He just looked at her with his caramel eyes turned hard candy.

"Delaware County Community College. I took a few classes when I started my own business."

A long moment passed while he considered her. "How are you doing with money? Are you in financial trouble? Any kind of trouble?"

"How are *you* doing with money? Is this going anywhere?" Her blood pressure was inching up. "And, hello? My house was blown up, and the FBI thinks I'm armed and dangerous. Of course I'm in trouble."

She wasn't sure if she caught a moment of hesitation in his body language or if she'd just imagined it. A long moment passed before he put forth his next question. "How well do you know your nephew?"

"Very. I've known him since he was born." She felt her defenses harden like a shell around her. He was going too far. "Leave my family out of whatever paranoia you are weaving here."

"How good is your nephew with computers?"

"He's a genius. He's been taking college-level courses since sixth grade. We're all very proud of him. He's already been offered a full scholarship to MIT."

"Sonuvabitch," he said under his breath, looking decidedly unhappy at the news. "Has he ever gotten in trouble?"

What did Zak's personal history have to do with anything? "Kids will be kids."

"What happened?"

"Why do you want to know?" She was getting the distinct sense that she was being interrogated—he'd put that gun on the table intentionally. Was he trying to intimidate her? After he'd spent the day convincing her that she shouldn't be scared of him, and after she'd finally believed it? After they'd kissed?

"Bailey," he growled.

Definitely trying to intimidate her.

Oh, fine. Let him have his stupid answers so they could finish this hundred-questions game already. "He hacked into the school server once and changed his English grade. He's not that good at composition." For heaven's sake, nobody could expect him to be a genius at absolutely everything. "He was punished, and he hasn't done anything since. He's a good kid." She emphasized that last part.

Cade leaned back in his chair without taking his gaze off her for a moment, his lips set in a tight line.

"Could you please tell me what this is about? Did the FBI question him and my brother? Did they say anything?" She was getting worried. And more than a little mad. What right did he have to question her like this, anyway?

"It's not fair that they should have to go through all this and be all upset because of *your* enemies. I know you didn't mean for any of this to happen, but I don't want my family involved in this. You don't know what they've been through already. Zak is a really good kid. He needs a break."

Cade closed his eyes for a second. "There's a good chance that he's selling weapons to terrorists."

"Who?" What on earth was he talking about?

But instead of answering her, he dialed his cell phone. "Where does your brother live? What's his name?"

"Bob." She gave him the address with some reluctance and listened as he talked to whomever he'd called.

"Could you do me a favor? I need you to pick up Bob and Zak Preston." He repeated the address she'd given him. "As fast as you can. Someplace safe. And take your brilliant wife with you. She's going to have some questions for the kid."

"Who was that?" she asked when he hung up. "You need to explain all this to me." She stood. To hell with the gun. They were talking about her family. "I want the truth and I want it now." He couldn't have meant what he'd said about Zak and weapons. He was just trying to scare her. But why? Total confusion reigned in her mind.

"That was a friend I trust."

"Is my family in danger because my house blew up? Because of me?" She felt the blood drain out of her head. If anything happened to Bob or Zak, she could never forgive herself.

She should have known something was off with her new neighbor. She'd known he was strange. But she'd written off his oddities as simply annoying. She should have been more vigilant. She should have known somehow that he wasn't just an ordinary man. She should have moved away. Should have, would have, could have…

"Because of you and whatever it is that you do, our house has been blown up." She was losing control of her anger. "And because of that, I'm now connected to *your* shady past. And because of that, my family is in danger!"

"Try the other way around." His expression turned even grimmer. "We're in danger because of them."

AN HOUR LATER, BAILEY'S head was still spinning, and she wasn't any closer to believing the nonsense Cade was telling her.

"Impossible."

"It's a fact. It was done on your PC. So you tell me. It's either you or Zak."

"You had me help you steal my own hard drive from the FBI so you could investigate me and get incriminating evidence in a domestic terrorism case. And all the while you pretended you were trying to help and protect me!"

If he hadn't put the gun back in his waistband, she would have been tempted to go for it. Maybe she should, anyway.

"If you were guilty, you're damn right I would have done anything to get proof and bring you in." To be fair, he didn't look too happy about it. "I was hoping I'd be wrong. Believe me, I didn't expect this."

The wheels in her mind were spinning like her handmade whirligigs.

Zak. Oh, God. "Zak can't possibly have a weapon. You don't know him. He's not like that."

"Someone could be using him to send precoded communications. He might not even know what he's doing. Does he have a part-time job that has to do with computers?"

"He's too young for a job."

"Doesn't mean he's not taking on some online work and getting paid via PayPal or something like that. It'd be easy enough for him to fudge his age in cyberspace. Does he seem to have too much pocket money?"

"I don't know. Not that I've seen." She didn't want to tell him more, afraid that any information she revealed he'd try to use against Zak. But if Zak was in trouble, they had to help him. And Cade was her best hope. Her only hope.

"We are not as close as we used to be." She had to tell him. "But I know that for a while he was obsessed with terrorists and how they communicated, what they wanted, how they did what they did. But just because of 9/11. He'd been through hell. He would never do anything to help them. If you knew him, you would know how ridiculous the thought is."

"He might not have been aware of what he was doing, Bailey."

She didn't know what to say to that. Zak was such an unreachable kid—had been for years. It was hard to say what went on in that supersmart head of his. Could he be tricked? In some ways, he *was* naive. Still, though he might have lacked social skills, when it came to his computer skills, he didn't lack confidence. He'd offered to automate her whole house when he'd arrived at the beginning of summer. She'd begged him not to, afraid that she wouldn't be able to keep things straight and would end up unable to turn on the lights.

In hindsight, she might have been better off giving him something like that to occupy himself. Maybe then he wouldn't have been trolling online for something to do.

The floor seemed to shift under her feet. If anything happened to Zak and Bob... They were the only close family she had. "Can I call them?"

"Not a good idea. I'll be notified when they're someplace safe. You'll have to make do with that for now."

"Thank you." She drew a deep breath. "I'm sorry about the things I said before." She'd berated him for dragging her into this situation when the truth was, she'd dragged him in.

She suddenly realized that he could walk away. She stilled as a million thoughts ran through her head, each more confusing and frightening than the one before it.

He had nothing to do with this.

Nothing. He could leave her to deal with all this all on her own.

Which she couldn't. This was so far beyond her, she couldn't come up with one idea about extricating herself from the mess her nephew had gotten them into. She was too scared to go to the authorities and too inexperienced to even think about hiding from them.

She was talented at a great many things, but knowing how to run from the law and evade capture was not one of them. She'd never even gotten a parking ticket in her whole life. Besides, running only worked if she could figure out the truth behind what had happened and use that information to bargain with the FBI.

Fear tightened her throat. Cade might have annoyed her to no end, and his kisses might have scrambled her brain, but she felt safe with him. He was always prepared for everything, always knew what to do next. She had as much self-confidence as the next woman, but with terrorists and the FBI after her, she was pretty sure she wouldn't last a day on her own.

If he didn't have way more money than she did—she'd seen the thick roll of twenties in his bag—she would have considered paying him to help her out of this mess. To help Zak. As it was, she had nothing to bargain with.

Except…

He wanted her.

He had wanted her in the water—she'd felt the proof pressed against her belly.

She had wanted him. But that was now beside the point.

The point was, how far was she willing to go? What was she willing to give for her life and the life of her family?

She would give just about anything not to have to be scared of the terrorists who blew up their house. Cade had connections. From what she'd seen of him so far, she believed that he could protect her and her family better than anyone else, including law enforcement. Neither the police nor the FBI would assign long-term bodyguards to Zak. And there were people after them with grenade launchers. But if Cade could be persuaded to help…

She smiled weakly at the man who held all the cards.

"Don't insult either of us." The color of his eyes seemed to deepen.

Heat rushed to her face. Was she that obvious? She was both embarrassed and relieved. "So what next?" She clenched her hands in her lap. *Please don't leave.* He wouldn't do that to her, would he? He had kissed her.

As part of his cover.

She held her breath, waiting for his answer, which didn't come immediately. So he was thinking about staying. That was good. If she was lucky, he was thinking that after the rocky start they'd gotten, he was really starting to like her.

That kiss in the lake had to mean something. She offered a tentative smile, trusting that he wouldn't misinterpret it. She meant nothing crazy by it this time.

"You sit tight. I'm going home," he said.

Chapter Seven

She'd thought he was going to leave her. Just like that. Man, that ticked him off. Cade kept checking his rearview mirror as he headed back to Chadds Ford. What kind of jerk did she think he was? He had *never* left a man or woman behind, not when they'd been under heavy fire, not when land mines had been exploding around them.

Never.

The look on her face when he'd said he was going home was insulting. Bailey Preston had a unique ability to get under his skin. In more ways than one.

He turned the car he'd boosted from a rental complex and got off Route 1, taking side streets.

Bailey Preston. He tapped on the steering wheel.

She was hot, but so were a million other women out there. He liked the fighting spirit in her, even if most of the time it annoyed him. He liked that she cared about her family. She was pretty strong, too—she'd taken the events of the past twenty-four hours in stride. She hadn't thrown a fit, hadn't freaked out, hadn't fallen apart.

But she had interfered with his thought processes, and that had to stop. He couldn't be thinking about the way her clothes hugged her curves when he was going into a night op. He pushed Bailey from his mind and tried to focus on his mission.

By the time he pulled onto their street, it was nearly dawn. He scanned the neighborhood for any sign that someone was waiting for him here, driving right by the mess that had been their duplex, police tape waving in the breeze around it. Her garden art lay scattered around the front yard, and he had an odd impulse to salvage a kooky sunflower or two, which was a really bad idea. He shouldn't go near the house.

So he was attracted to Bailey. Had kissed her. Twice. They were consenting adults.

Maybe that had been the source of the frustration between them all along: denied attraction. Easy enough to fix.

He turned down the next cul-de-sac and pulled up to the first house on the left. The driveway stood empty. No lights on inside. He rolled up the driveway into the cover of the garage, safe from the windows. Then he let the engine idle while he got out and stole to the shed that stood halfway between his house and the neighbor's. Nothing looked disturbed around his hiding place. Good. He eased out a carefully sawed section of a railroad tie that supported the shed and then pulled out the lockbox he'd hid inside a month ago.

He carefully fitted the chunk of wood back in

place. Thirty more seconds and he was out of there. He was heading back to the car with the box under his arm when he spotted movement in the ruins of his house. Could be the wind playing with a piece of rubble. Could be a cat. He pulled into the shadows and stopped to watch.

But it was neither. Someone emerged and glanced around before taking off across the lawns. Cade got into the car and followed, hoping to catch another glimpse. Maybe it was just a looting teenager from the neighborhood.

He was passing the entrance to his own street when he heard a car start up somewhere down the lane. He pulled over, turned the car off and ducked down. Less than a minute passed before a dark pickup rolled by him, heading in the other direction. He gave it some lead before he followed.

Four in the morning was the absolute worst time to tail a man. There was no traffic on the roads. He had to stay way back, then run red lights to catch up. Which worked until he came upon a police cruiser by the side of the road and was forced to sit out a light. He was wanted by the FBI, driving a stolen car and in possession of an unregistered firearm. Better not give the cops an excuse to pull him over.

By the time the light turned, the guy had disappeared onto one of the side streets heading toward a shopping complex. Cade drove around in that area for another hour, but he didn't spot the pickup again.

So the guy wasn't just a neighborhood teen rummaging through the ruins out of curiosity. Nor would he be from the FBI or the police. They could—and certainly had—searched the house during daylight hours. That left the bastards who'd blown up his home.

He watched the street carefully, scanning the shadows. Most of what he could see was deserted. A few delivery trucks went about their early morning business, going around a handful of bleary-eyed travelers in a white sedan parked at a fast-food restaurant. Still, something didn't feel right. He had half a mind to park and do a building by building search. Except that he didn't want to leave Bailey alone anymore. He'd already been gone longer than he'd planned. He swore and turned his car toward Maryland.

He was crossing the state border just as the first ray of the sun came over the horizon. Frustration hummed in his veins. He'd tagged a tango but lost him. Everything was so much simpler in the jungle or the mountains of Afghanistan. No cops to hold you back when you were going after the enemy. If it weren't for them, he could have pulled his gun and clipped the guy from the back.

Some days, civilian life was all right. Like when he mowed the lawn and watched Bailey through her open garage door as she painted daisies on weatherproof canvas. But other days, he wouldn't have minded a little more action.

The miles ticked by, and eventually his mind turned to another kind of action as he thought of Bailey, waiting for him in bed.

BAILEY WAS SLEEPING fitfully, alone in the shack. Her mind kept playing the "Hottest Moments with Cade Palmer" video montage in her head. Played, replayed and embellished.

They were in the water again. He kissed her. My, oh my, did he kiss her. His mouth was firm and hot and all-knowing. And he didn't stop there. He kissed her neck, pulled the T-shirt over her head and trailed his lips over her feverish skin. His arms encircled her, and he lifted her until her legs were wrapped around his waist, their bodies aligned. She moaned.

She didn't know whether she had woken herself up, or the man who was sitting at the plastic table had done it. Her heart lurched into a panic for a split second before she recognized Cade.

He'd come back. Not that she had doubted that he would, not after he promised to see this to the end. But it had been a long night all alone.

He watched her without saying a word.

Her heart switched to a whole other rhythm.

Could be a good time for the bedclothes to swallow her up. Had she moaned out loud? And if she had, would he know what she'd been dreaming about?

"Sorry I woke you." His voice was low and rough when he finally spoke.

She suddenly realized that the sheets had slipped off and her T-shirt had ridden up on her torso. Her stomach and the underside of her breasts were showing. She yanked the T-shirt back into place and sat up, making sure the sheet covered her completely.

Didn't seem to make any difference to him. He was still staring her down.

Oh. She *had* moaned out loud!

Heat crept to her cheeks. At least he wouldn't see that. He hadn't turned on the light, and the early morning sun coming in through the single window only lit the place dimly.

"Did you just get in?" Her voice was scratchy.

He nodded. She took a deep breath.

"Did I talk in my sleep?" Better to know than to drive herself nuts over it.

"Slept like an angel." He stood and moved toward the bed.

Her mouth went dry. She almost asked what he thought he was doing and then realized that he would be going to sleep. Of course. He'd been up all night. He would need some rest. She scooted to the side, swinging her legs over the edge.

"Stay." The single word was spoken softly, as a request.

And in truth, she couldn't have moved for a cash bonus as he dropped to the futon next to her, the mattress dipping under his weight.

"How did it go?" *Keep it businesslike. Nothing personal.*

"Got what I went for." He folded his hands under his head.

His weapon stash. He'd told her that he needed a few things to complement what he was borrowing from Joey.

"The house?" She tried not to be too obvious

about staring at his bulging biceps. Even the dim light couldn't diminish those.

"Pretty much the same as when we left. Plus some police tape. And a visitor."

She pulled her legs back on the bed and folded them under herself so she could fully turn toward him. "Who?"

"I'm guessing a tango. Terrorist."

He'd been in danger. On her behalf. While she slept.

On one level, if anyone could take care of himself, it was Cade. He sure didn't need her watching his back. But it still didn't feel right.

"Later today I want to go back to the area where I lost him and check around again." He looked tired and grim. Something else was bothering him, something he wasn't telling her about.

"Can I come?"

He didn't respond.

She had a feeling he didn't particularly want her as backup. Tough. She was all he had right now. "I'd rather not stay here alone again." Which was the truth. "While you were gone, I kept wondering what would happen if someone found me here." She played the helpless female card with distaste. But she knew what she wanted, and she was willing to play even dirtier tricks than that.

"Okay."

"Really?" She had expected to have to fight him on this one.

He closed his eyes.

She lay back down, facing him. "You think we're going to make it? Find a way out of this?"

"You bet," he said.

"How?" Try as she might, she could not see the light at the end of the tunnel. Not even a pinprick. "If Zak is somehow involved in this… The FBI can't arrest a teenager, can they?"

"They can and they will. According to them, he established and maintained contact with known terrorists. It'd take a while for him to explain his way out of that one and convince Homeland Security that it was a game or a misunderstanding. They'd be riding him and riding him hard. I'd rather that he didn't have to go through that. Considering his past."

Her throat closed up, her chest heavy with the thought that he cared about a boy he'd barely met. "Thank you." The words came out on a whisper.

He turned toward her then and opened his eyes. Their rich caramel color gave way to burnished gold in the early morning light. "You don't have to be so surprised every time I do something that doesn't confirm your notion that I'm a complete bastard." He sounded tired.

"I don't…" But the truth was, she had thought him an annoying jerk for the past three months and had cursed the day when he had inherited the other half of the duplex. It was becoming obvious now that she hadn't really known her new neighbor at all. "Sorry."

"Don't worry about it." He turned his whole body so they were face-to-face, with only a few inches of empty space between them. "I want to know exactly who is after Zak and how he got tricked into whatever he got tricked into. If I get them and hand them over, it would greatly simplify things for us. Not that Zak still won't catch plenty of flack. I want you to prepare for that. Carly will prep him for questioning—she knows firsthand what he needs to say. But whichever way this goes down, it won't be a walk in the park."

Her mind was stuck on *get them*. "We are going to hunt—" how had he put it? "—known terrorists?"

"Hunt and catch the bastards." He actually grinned. Then slowly, the grin slid off his face as he held her gaze and closed the distance between them.

SHE LOOKED LIKE SHE WAS about to freak out over the terrorist thing. He had to distract her somehow. At least that was what he told himself. Mostly he had to slake the hunger he'd worked up for her while he'd been gone, while he'd watched her sleep on that bed, her flat stomach and the tantalizing curves of her breasts calling to him across the dim room.

He'd gone from bone tired to fully aroused in under sixty seconds after walking through the door. He'd parked his ass in the chair farthest from the bed and made himself stay there. But the small moan that had escaped her just before she'd awoken had done him in.

He kissed her with all his built-up need. Her lips were soft and yielding, her body pliant against his. It wasn't going to be one of those "he meant only to kiss her and then got carried away" moments. He'd meant—from the time he'd walked in the door and seen her tangled in the sheets—to make her fully his. As long as she had no objections. And from the way she was kissing him back, she sure didn't seem like she had any.

"You drive me crazy," he murmured against her mouth, and meant it not only in the way of the senses.

"Ditto."

Being in bed with her like this was beyond strange after they'd spent the first three months of knowing each other bickering endlessly. They were definitely primed for the moment, however. He was reaching for her T-shirt just as she reached for his.

Her skin was warm velvet, waiting to be explored.

"If you don't want to see this through, you might want to let me know now," he said, his face pressed against her neck. A screeching halt two inches from the finish line might give him a heart attack.

"I want…" Her words dissolved into a moan that made him want to sprint for that finish line ASAP, but what little sense he had left said the moment should be savored.

"I want, too," he said, his mouth around a nipple that was tightening into a hard nub.

Good to know that she wasn't immune to him, either.

Her panties slipped off so fast, it was as if they were running away on their own. He made quick work of his jeans and boxers next.

The sensation of lying skin to skin with her was exquisite torture. He couldn't stop his roaming hands. He loved the swell of her breasts, the curve of her hips, the moist heat between her legs.

She moaned again when he slipped a finger in to explore that particular spot. She arched her back, which made her breasts press harder against his chest, her nipples rubbing against him. He bent again to latch on to one, then the other, and held her in place as she writhed on the bed.

She was beautiful and sweet and responsive, and she was driving him wild. He waited until he felt the first tremors build inside her before he pulled away. "Give me a sec."

He strode to the bathroom—a man on a mission—and dug out Joey's first-aid kit from under the sink, grabbing one of the foil packs and hurrying back to the bed.

She had pulled the sheet over herself, but he snatched it away. Then he was next to her, on her, between her legs. He kissed her as he entered her in one smooth slide, all the way. And nearly went blind from the pleasure of it.

They should have done this sooner. Much sooner. Like the day he'd moved in. A much better way of dealing with the energy between them than fighting.

Hello, I'm your new neighbor. Care to come to bed? Okay, maybe it wouldn't have worked quite like that.

He eased out, then in again, then lost all ability to think. Their past disappeared; the shack disappeared; he couldn't even see the futon anymore, just her violet eyes going unfocused as she arched her back and whispered his name. Her legs wrapped around his waist as he pumped deep inside, her heels digging into his backside, pulling him in. He obliged her and went deeper yet.

After they soared off into space together and came back down to earth, he collapsed next to her, his mind blank from pleasure, his breath ragged. She tried to slip out of bed.

With his last ounce of energy, he pulled her back to him. "Stay. Please."

And at first, his dreams were pleasant. But soon he was in the rain forest, back in the killing, then in Jakarta again. Pachaimani was standing in front of the back gate of the compound. "When are you coming back?" he said.

Cade woke saying his name.

"Who is that?" Bailey was watching him. "Is he the boy you mentioned before?"

His mouth was too dry to say anything, so he just nodded.

"Friend of yours?"

He swallowed to wet his tongue.

"Your son?" Her eyes went wide.

He wished. "He used to be a connection." An asset. He worked for a man the United States had targeted, a suspected terror financier.

"I thought you said he was just a kid."

"Ten years old and as good a spy as I ever met." He grinned. Boy, he was quick both in the mind and on his feet. Industrious, too. Could talk himself out of just about any trouble. Reminded him of Matthew, the younger brother he'd lost to leukemia at about the same age.

"You're a spy?" Her eyes went wider yet, but she held up a hand the next second. "No. Don't say 'kind of.' Just don't say anything. There are spy kids, like the movie, for real?"

Hardly like the movie. There'd been no gadgets involved, no glamour. "Think Indonesia, not Hollywood. When Pachaimani was nine, almost his whole family was murdered in front of him. His brothers and sisters raped, then mutilated." What in hell was he thinking? He shouldn't be telling her this. It wasn't a story fit for her ears—for anyone's.

"What happened?"

He shouldn't have gone on, but he did, maybe to remind himself he still needed to keep the promise he made to Pachaimani. "His father had worked for a man known only as Ruvaraj, which means 'prince.' Pachi's father was accused of stealing food for his wife and seven kids. They were all put to death except Pachaimani and his six-year-old sister. Pachaimani was made to watch, then forced into servitude, slavery really, to take his father's place. And his sister was sold."

"How did you meet him?"

He was gathering intelligence on Ruvaraj. Pachaimani helped him, risking his own life. He lived for one reason only: to grow strong enough to avenge his family, to find his sister and kill Ruvaraj. Until Cade had promised to take care of Ruvaraj himself. He gave the kid some money and told him to forget revenge and run away the first chance he had.

But Pachaimani gave the money back and told

Cade that he wouldn't leave until he had his sister. And Ruvaraj was the connection. Only he knew where she was.

In some ways, Pachi was just like Matthew had been. Didn't know the meaning of the word *impossible*. But he had little innocence left after living through what had been done to his family, and surviving day to day inside Ruvaraj's compound. He had the heart of a soldier.

It wasn't a story he wanted to tell anyone—not even Bailey. "I used to work all over the place. The world is full of tragedies," he said and pulled her to him, wrapping his arms around her sweet warmth and closing his eyes. "Five more minutes," he said.

WHEN HE WOKE AGAIN, the sun was high enough to shine through the window. He'd slept better and felt better than he had in a long time. He stayed still after opening his eyes, breathing in the scent of Bailey's skin, soaking in her presence.

He'd learned to appreciate good moments like this, to stop and enjoy them. They were few and far between in a life like his. He'd fallen asleep right after they had made love, so he basked now in the late glow of those incredible moments.

He glanced down at Bailey and noticed she had a funny look in her eyes as she gazed at him. It brought him back from the edge of drifting off again. She looked…dreamy.

Very unlike Bailey. Since they'd met, for the most part, she'd been frowning at him nonstop.

Whoa. *The* look?

He snapped out of his bliss, sensing danger all around all of a sudden.

Dammit. He should have thought about that last night, before he'd gone all crazy with her body. He hadn't lost control so completely in… He couldn't even remember the last time.

And *then* he remembered he'd told her about Pachi. Confided in her. Women always put a lot of stock in that.

Unease skittered along his skin. Damage control, that was what he needed, and fast. He drew a slow breath. "Okay. Don't get mad. What I'm about to say, I'm saying for your own good."

He didn't want her to get hurt. He was really starting to like her. A lot.

"Oh." She pulled the sheet to her chin and drew back a few inches. "Was it that bad? It's been a while, and I—" Pink tinged her cheeks. She looked away.

"If you were any better, I'd be dead." He ran his hand down her arm and felt a stirring under his own part of the sheet, but repressed it ruthlessly. "Bailey?"

Her gaze returned reluctantly to his.

"What I was about to say was, don't do something crazy and fall for me." He paused. "You're great. I love spending time with you. This is just not going to go that way."

He expected her to be mad. To have to appease her. But he had taken that risk because he wanted to be honest with her.

Instead, relief washed across her beautiful face, and she laughed. "I don't believe in love."

She had to be joking. Women always believed in love. If anything, they were overly sentimental about it.

"Okay." Whatever she said.

"You believe in love?" She had an odd look on her face now, like she was humoring him.

What—she didn't think him capable of emotion? So much for that comfortable postcoital glow. She was really starting to annoy him. Again. Which was good, actually. Better than whatever strangeness was developing between them.

He moved from the bed and pulled his jeans on. "I'll go and look around outside."

"Do you believe in falling in love?" she insisted, with a good dose of skepticism in her voice.

"Of course, I do. I just don't plan on doing it," he said.

Chapter Eight

They were deep in the woods on the other side of the lake. The early afternoon sun played hide-and-seek with the leaves, the silence of the forest a palpable presence. She should have felt peace; instead, she felt out of sorts that Cade would think she would fall stupid in love with him over great sex. The best she had ever had, but still. She hadn't grown up on romance novels. She'd spent her teenage years in court, along with her brother, the subject of drawn-out custody battles.

Cade stepped behind her, lifted his gun and pressed it into her right hand, helping her to bring it up. He moved closer, completely closing the distance between them so she could brace her back on his wide chest. The top of her head barely reached his chin. He guided her hand and the gun, aiming at the makeshift target he'd put up.

"Okay, everything's lined up?"

Hard to say when she was feeling cross-eyed from his nearness. The peace of the small clearing seemed filled with heavy air all of a sudden. Need, passion, desire. Images of their lovemaking at dawn would not leave her mind.

His love-babbling nonsense aside, they did have great sex. Wow.

Her handful of previous relationships hadn't prepared her for Cade. She had spoken the truth when she'd told him that she didn't believe in love. Which didn't mean that she was a thirty-five-year-old virgin.

She dated. As long as it was fun for both parties. When that changed, she left. She couldn't say she had regrets, that she had ever once looked back after walking away.

But she'd never met a man who caused the kind of instant tension, instant awareness that Cade did. There had been times when she wanted to strangle her ornery new neighbor. Then there had been times when she woke from dreams of him that left her groaning with frustration. But this morning had not been a dream. And she was still wired from it. A tingle ran across her skin.

"Ready?"

Was she ever. She blinked her eyes, focused on the crosshairs and pulled the trigger.

"Not bad." He stepped back, and she missed his steady presence. "You hit the paper."

Barely. "Are you sure I need to learn this?"

He flashed her a "come on, now" look. "Let's take ten steps closer."

This time he did not hold her from behind. Too

bad. She took her shot. The bullet hit much closer to the middle of the target.

"Are you going to tell me to wait until I see the whites of their eyes?" She looked over her shoulder, into his handsome face.

He smiled. "Hell, no. If the situation gets to the point where shots are being fired, shoot at anything that moves."

He made her practice with a few more rounds, then called a halt and picked up their spent shells before taking down the old newspaper he'd tacked to a tree. "We should get going. Try not to worry about this stuff too much. You'll be staying in the car. I'm not planning on taking you into danger."

"Good to know. Do you—"

He answered his chirping phone. "What's up?" He listened for a while. "Okay. Keep looking."

"Who was that?" she asked after he'd hung up.

"They picked up your brother. He is in a safe place." He held her gaze, and there was something in his caramel eyes that made the breath catch in her chest.

"Zak?" Her fingertips went numb. She wanted him to go on but was scared of what he might say.

He seemed reluctant to answer but then opened his mouth after an endless moment or two. "He's disappeared. Left for school yesterday but never got there. His cell is turned off."

Her knees began to shake. The only thing she could think of was that after the first twenty-four hours, the chances of finding a missing person dropped rapidly. And Zak had been missing for twenty-four hours already, without her even knowing it. He could already be—

He was by her side the next second, a supporting arm around her waist as he pulled her to him. "Take it easy. He's a teenager. Could be he got ticked over something and took off. He's probably holed up at a friend's house."

"Or in the hands of bloodthirsty terrorists." She blinked rapidly. She couldn't bear to think about Zak in danger. He was her baby nephew. He'd been a little butterball of a kid at the beginning, and then a precocious toddler who'd declared Aunt Bailey his favorite. Then came school, the age of being a "big boy." Then 9/11, after which nobody had been able to truly reach him, followed speedily by an increasingly introverted adolescence.

"The bad guys couldn't have figured out that he was the one who sent the messages, could they?"

He rested his head on her chin. "I don't know. But I'm going to get some answers. I promise."

She could feel his voice vibrate up the strong column of his neck as she breathed in his masculine scent and let it comfort her. He pressed a featherlight kiss to her forehead.

"I should have spent more time with him while he was with me. I could have tried harder." But she'd been hurt by him shutting her out almost completely. She'd felt sharply the rejection of him saying no to every suggestion she'd made, be it going to the movies, for a hike or to the Philadelphia Zoo.

"It's hard to get to know someone who doesn't

want to be known. He was dealing with his own stuff. You giving him a place to stay helped, I'm sure." His voice was gentle as he held her.

Their coming together in bed had been all about passion. She had understood that on a visceral level. She wasn't sure what to do with the overwhelming tenderness he was wrapping her up in now. She wanted to fall into it, to melt against his strength. And wanting that scared her. They were still little more than strangers, brought together by circumstance.

She didn't want to rely on him too much or get too far lost in the comfort he offered. Because when this was over, what would she do?

"We should get going. The sooner we find out more about this whole mess, the sooner we can help Zak if he's in trouble."

He took her hand and led her out of the woods. And she didn't have it in her to pull away, not even when she was concerned that he might have already softened something inside her without her noticing.

"We're in this together. If Zak is in trouble, we are going to get him out," he said.

She squeezed his hand, unable to stop herself. He squeezed back.

We are in this together. Bailey was still thinking about those words two hours later when they were circling the neighborhood—for the fourth time—where Cade had lost his man last night.

Fast-food restaurants. Jo-Ann's Fabrics. Optometrist. Hairdresser. Gift shop. Small convenience store.

Furniture rental. Blockbuster. And so on and so forth, a plethora of small stores lining their way. People were conducting their business: mothers with their kids, senior citizens, a couple of teenagers. At midafternoon, the schools were just getting out. The office crowd was still firmly trapped in their cubicles.

We're in this together. She hadn't heard those words many times in her life, not from her mother, and certainly not from her father. Both had looked at their kids as weapons to use against each other during and after a bitter divorce. The only person she'd ever been able to count on was her brother, Bobby. He must be going crazy with Zak missing.

"Can I call my brother?" she asked.

"Not a good idea." Cade kept his gaze on the people and the cars. "He's at a safe house. It's better not to have any communications for the time being."

She hated that but saw his point. "Okay."

"What do you know about that place?" He nodded toward an abandoned and boarded-up restaurant. Faded lettering on the window advertised lunch specials.

"It's been closed forever."

"So why do you think there's a camera above the door?" he asked.

She looked at the black security camera, which was recording passing traffic. The small electronic device blended nearly perfectly into the shadows above the door. If Cade hadn't pointed it out, she wouldn't have spotted it in a million years.

"It's not a high-crime area. Why would a restaurant that's been empty for a while need security like that?" He passed without slowing down.

Her heartbeat picked up speed. She hadn't expected anything from today's search. Sure, some guy Cade had followed the night before had been here. And Cade insisted that he wouldn't have lost the guy, if he hadn't pulled in someplace. But she hadn't been so sure. She routinely got lost caravanning to the shore with her coworkers in the summer—it was too easy for cars to get between them, or for her to not pay attention for a second and lose the car she was following.

But Cade was right about the camera. Definitely strange.

"What do we do now?"

"Check out the place from the back." He circled around and went down a service alley.

They identified the back of the restaurant by its name printed on the brick wall that separated it from the alley. She stared at the new-looking barbed wire on top of the wall. This was Chadds Ford, a ritzy, historical district where people had maids, gardeners and nannies. You didn't see all that much barbed wire around.

"They want to keep people out. I'm thinking it's not just to protect some secret recipe."

She was beginning to think the same.

A dark van appeared at the end of the alleyway, coming head-on. Cade kept on moving, then pulled all the way to the shoulder so it could pass them. They watched in the rearview mirror as the van stopped in front of the restaurant's back gate. The gate slid open, and the van disappeared behind it.

"Closed restaurants don't take deliveries." Fear balled in her stomach. It was one thing to say they were going after the bad guys—it was another to be arm's length from them.

There were terrorists. In her hometown. Who had blown up her house and had possibly taken her nephew. Seeing the van brought the point home, made it feel more real than before. All this time, she'd been hoping this whole fiasco was just a series of accidents and misunderstandings. Denial was such a comforting place to be. She hated to have to let go of it completely, but faced with these latest developments, she had no choice.

"That's the van I saw in front of the house just before it blew." Cade's lips flattened into a grim line.

The ball of fear expanded in her stomach.

"Should we call the police now? Or the FBI?" She was rapidly losing confidence. This was already a lot closer than she'd ever wanted to get to this kind of business.

Cade parked at the end of the alleyway and pulled out of sight from the restaurant's back entry. "You stay here. I'm going in."

Their plan to go after the bad guys suddenly looked like a real bad idea. "Are you sure?"

"I have to look around."

"At least take your stash."

He had his bag of tricks in the trunk, along with weaponry from Joey.

"This should be enough." He patted the handgun tucked into the back of his waistband. "You got your weapon ready?"

She nodded. Unlike him, having a weapon didn't make her feel any better. Made her feel more nervous, in fact.

"Use it only if you feel that your life is in danger. But if it is, don't hesitate. Otherwise, no heroics." He pressed a quick kiss on her lips, then was gone the next second.

Gone, gone. Over a fence. So no one driving down the alleyway would see him, she supposed. He was going to sneak through the backyards of several local businesses. And she was going to sit here and go quietly crazy.

Except that she couldn't, not beyond five minutes. She had to at least get out of the car and move. She would walk up the side street. He hadn't said she couldn't. She was in a shopping area. A woman walking around shouldn't rouse anyone's suspicions.

She double-checked her weapon to make sure the safety was on, then tucked it into her waistband like she'd seen him do. It felt funny, carrying that big lump at the small of her back. She checked in the side mirror when she got out. Not too bad. The folds of her shirt covered it fine.

She walked a few tentative steps, expecting the gun to fall down her pant leg any second, then walked more securely once she realized that wasn't going to happen. She glanced into the alleyway as she passed it. Nothing. She couldn't see Cade scaling fences. Could he be at his destination already?

She'd reached Jo-Ann's Fabrics, but she could barely see what was in the window. Her mind couldn't focus on anything but what Cade might be doing and where Zak could possibly be. He had disappeared in New York. The police were looking for him. She didn't want to think of all the children who disappeared in New York City in any given year and were never found.

She heard a car door slam behind her and spun around to look at the Avalon Cade had boosted for today's mission. Nobody there. Had the noise come from the alleyway? She strolled back that way, as if she'd forgotten something in her car.

Another van stood in front of the back gate of the restaurant, this one white. She couldn't see anybody. Whoever had driven it must have gone in.

She wished she could warn Cade. She looked at the van's New Jersey license plate and memorized the numbers. There wasn't much else she could do at the moment. She walked back to the Avalon, got in and rolled her window down to make sure she could hear any noise coming from the restaurant.

It wasn't long before she did. A pop. A car backfiring? A gunshot? It didn't sound like the shots she'd fired when she'd been target shooting, but back then the gun was going off right next to her. She had no idea what a gunshot would sound like from a distance.

She made sure her weapon was secure, then got out of the car again and walked up the line of shops.

She walked all the way this time, passing the restaurant. She could see nothing through the darkened window, no sign of life inside.

Except the door was ajar a fraction of an inch. Had it been that way when they'd driven by? She might not have noticed, but she had a feeling that Cade would have. He was a man for detail.

What if it *had* been a gunshot? What if he was in there, in trouble? She walked on, but turned at the next corner and came back. This time she hesitated in front of the door. She could just push it open and stick her head in. If anyone was in there, she would pretend that she wanted to know if they were reopening.

Of course, there was the camera, continuously scanning. Except that it was pointed up the street right now. She quickly stepped forward, as close to the door as possible, where hopefully the camera wouldn't be able to see her.

The hinges didn't make a sound as she inched the door open, and she gave heaven thanks for that.

The main dining room was dark. Chairs were stacked on the tables, the floor dusty except for a path leading to the kitchen in the back, spiderwebs hanging from the ceiling. Didn't look like the place had seen a cleaning crew since it had closed abruptly a few months back.

There was a strange, stale smell in the air which permeated everything. She followed the path back to the kitchen, walking past a professional-size refrigerator and stepping on a large, dark stain on the tile floor where something had leaked out of the fridge. The dank odor was even stronger here.

Had the owners left in such a great hurry that they didn't even clean out the food before they moved on? Were they pushed out by some terrorist cell who wanted to take over their location? Or were they involved in it all?

She opened the fridge out of curiosity, thinking that any clue might be useful. Cade was probably scouting the back, too busy with the men who'd come in the vans. It was unlikely he would even make it all the way up here.

As soon as she cracked the refrigerator seal, she knew she'd made a mistake. She gagged, shoving the door closed again, but not before she caught sight of the blackened corpse inside.

Fighting the urge to either scream, faint or puke her guts out, she felt her heart just about stop when a hand clamped over her mouth.

"What do you think you're doing in here?" Cade whispered, his tone low and none too happy.

But before she could answer, voices came from the far end of the room. People were coming. Cade whirled her toward a cleaning closet and squeezed in there with her, placing himself in front. He didn't have to tell her to be quiet.

Men came into the kitchen, about a half dozen of them, judging from their voices. They spoke a language she didn't understand. They were fighting—that, at least, was clear.

Broom and mop handles stuck in her back. She

was plastered against Cade's wide shoulders. His presence was reassuring in a situation that made her want to jump out of her skin. She was no longer scared—she'd crossed over to petrified, as in physically hurting with fear, her lungs too tight to breathe in air; her muscles were clenched so tight that they cramped. She could think of little else but the terrorists outside the closet and the corpse in the fridge next to it. If it weren't for Cade, she might have passed out or started shaking hard enough to betray her hiding place.

Should have stayed in the car. She could have cried, she was so mad at herself. What on earth had she been thinking?

She struggled for air, waiting to be discovered at any second. But the men went on and on, talking and not doing much else. Chairs slid around the tile floor. Was the kitchen their meeting place? Didn't the dead body bother them? If this place had been their headquarters for a while, surely they had noticed the corpse and its stench. She could still smell it, even in the closet, her stomach rolling with nausea. She pressed her nose into Cade's back and inhaled his scent.

Steps neared. The closet door creaked. She nearly peed her pants. Then, after a breathless moment, she realized that one of the men had leaned against their door.

Cade shifted soundlessly, extended his left hand back, took her hand and wrapped her arm around his chest. His heartbeat was steady and strong. He kept his hand on top of hers—a gesture of comfort and tenderness. She needed both badly at the moment. Then she realized it might not be a gesture of comfort at all. Maybe he was saying goodbye. Maybe it was the sort of gesture that said, *Let me hold you one more time before we die.*

HE DIDN'T LIKE THE situation he was in, not with Bailey there next to him. Apparently, he hadn't been clear when he'd told her to stay out of trouble. Next time he was handcuffing her to the steering wheel.

They weren't exactly in an easily defendable position. They were sitting ducks in that closet. Their best bet was to remain undiscovered. Man, the stench was bad. Brought back memories of his first mission to Colombia, where he'd been caught by a local warlord and tossed into a dungeon. He'd had a roommate, a crazy Russian who died from his injuries. They never bothered to remove him. Sergey was still there when Cade finally broke out a month later, not that far from death himself.

He'd had trouble with being locked up since, one of the reasons why he wasn't willing to give himself up to the FBI and wait in a cell until they cleared him.

Bailey pressed tight against his back, distracting him from the past, and from the tangos in the kitchen who were bickering over funds that hadn't arrived. And complaining about American coffee. He didn't speak fluent Arabic, but he understood more than enough to get the gist.

A door creaked to his left. Probably the same one that he'd come through earlier.

"Any news from New York?" The speaker's voice held authority.

The others immediately quieted.

"Not yet," somebody said.

"If we can't get the weapon today or tomorrow, we'll have to go with our other plan." The boss's voice held undisguised anger.

"It's a good plan," someone volunteered. "We are ready."

"And your martyrdom is appreciated. But this time we don't want anyone to tie the crash back to us. The weapon would allow us to destroy our enemies without leaving a trace," the boss said.

The Arabic language had many dialects. Cade was most familiar with the one that was spoken in Southeast Asia, where he'd completed a number of missions. This man's dialect sounded a lot like that of people Cade knew from Nigeria. Similar but not the same. Maybe from somewhere farther south?

"Our cause is worthy. If we make the ultimate sacrifice, it will be remembered. But I'm not one to think it righteous to waste a human life if it isn't absolutely necessary."

A couple of men murmured their agreement. There seemed to be a solemnity to the occasion, a hush that came over the room outside. It made Cade's skin crawl and his finger itch on the trigger.

Martyrdom and *crash*. Two words you didn't want to hear when eavesdropping on a terrorist group.

Cade shifted slightly. Not enough information to be useful, but more than enough to send the Department of Homeland Security into a frenzy.

If he could make it out of here and pass on the intelligence.

"The plane leaves tomorrow," the leader said. "We must be prepared."

"If we don't have the weapon by then, we'll be on the flight," another man added. Instead of sounding scared, he sounded wistful.

BAILEY DIDN'T UNDERSTAND a word that was being said outside their hiding place, but from the way Cade's body stiffened, she knew it couldn't be good. The men lounged around for nearly an hour before moving on. When several minutes passed with no noises filtering through the closet door, Cade pushed it open an inch.

He paused before opening the door fully. "All clear," he mouthed.

Bailey stepped out after him, her legs stiff from standing in the cramped space for so long. Her knees were weak from nervous exhaustion. If this day wouldn't make her go gray, nothing could.

"Where did you come in?" Cade was moving forward, gun in hand.

"Front. The door was open."

"You have your gun?"

She showed him.

"Okay. Go back that way. Sit in the car." He gave her a hard look. "Wait. For. Me. I mean it."

"And you?" She didn't want to sneak around this place alone, not since she'd seen the contents of the fridge. And she didn't want him to stay here alone, either.

"I'm taking a closer look. They were talking about a plane. I need more, something we can use to stop them."

He headed toward the kitchen's swinging door, looking through the round glass window. "You should be fine. There's nobody out there." He opened his cell phone.

"Who are you calling?"

"I got a few pictures before you came in. I'm passing them on to a friend to check them against some databases." He hit a series of buttons and slipped the phone back into his pocket. "If they have Zak, we'll find him." He pushed the door open and waited for her to pass through.

On impulse, she put her arms around him and squeezed before slipping through, and damn if she knew what *that* was about. Something had shifted between them, but she couldn't put her finger on when that had happened or what it was. And she didn't want to.

"Be careful," she whispered, hesitating on the other side of the door.

"You, too." He watched her with an unreadable look in his eyes.

Then he closed the door behind her, and she was alone in the large, dim room which looked fit to be haunted. She made her way to the front carefully, making sure she didn't knock against a table or a chair. But she did look back when she got to the door. Something dark had moved into the restaurant since she'd last been in here with friends from work. Something that had brought spiderwebs and emptiness and the stench of decay. A shiver ran down her spine.

Zak was somehow involved with this darkness, had been taken by it. He was just a kid, too smart for his own good. A kid with an exceptional brain who hadn't yet learned how to channel his energies and his talent. A kid who might never get a chance to do so. Her throat tightened at the thought. For a second, the image of the blackened corpse in the fridge crowded out everything else in her brain.

Oh, Zak. What have you done?

He'd done something crazy. Crazy wrong. He deserved to be shaken, to be scared straight, to be grounded until his twenty-first birthday. But he didn't deserve what these men might do to someone who crossed them.

She glanced back at the kitchen. Cade was there. Cade would help. The gruesome image of the corpse flashed into her mind again. It would take time to forget that. A sob escaped her, and she drew a breath, too deep. Her nose filled with that stale, sick smell, and she gagged.

She didn't hear the front door open behind her, so she was startled out of her skin when a gun pushed into her back.

Chapter Nine

Bailey's first instinct was to scream, but the hard, pointy object in her ribs shifted, and the next second she was hit hard enough on the back of the head to see stars. Her knees gave and the wave of nausea that'd been rising in her throat rolled over her.

Whoever had come in hooked his hands under her armpits and dragged her toward the kitchen.

Thank God. Thank God. Cade would be there.

But when they went through the swinging doors, Cade was nowhere to be seen. Panic engulfed her even in her stunned state. She could feel little, in fact, beyond pain and fear.

She might have blacked out for a while, because suddenly she found herself in a small, dark space, disoriented, unsure which way was up for a second. She was pressed against something fuzzy.

All she could think of was the corpse in the fridge.

She filled her lungs with dank air and screamed her head off, pushing wildly with her hands and kicking with her feet, hoping to open the door. Nothing gave.

She was interrupted by the sound of a car starting, and her place of confinement began to vibrate, then move. The stench of exhaust filled her nose.

Relief came so sharp it brought moisture to her eyes. She wasn't in the fridge, or buried alive. She was in the trunk of a car. She reached out. Her hand met not with hair, but with the carpeting in the trunk.

Her moment of relief passed quickly. She might not be in the fridge, but her situation was far from rosy. She had little doubt over who had taken her.

Calm down. Don't panic.

Too late for that. The fear rushed back all over again, but she fought it. She couldn't give up. If she did, she was as good as dead.

At least they hadn't shot her right off the bat. She was alive, and as long as she was alive, there was always the hope of rescue or escape, always a slim chance. Cade would soon be looking for her.

She wouldn't allow herself to think that he would have absolutely no way of knowing where they'd taken her.

CADE SEARCHED THROUGH the building methodically, avoiding the men who occupied it. At least six terrorists were upstairs, according to his best estimate. He started in the basement, in the storage rooms, but found nothing. No computers, no guns, no explosives, no documents.

Didn't look like the headquarters were in the abandoned restaurant. Maybe they used the place only for clandestine meetings. Possibly for meetings with people they didn't trust enough to take to the base of their operations. There had to be more than this somewhere else.

He made a thorough search, hoping he might find Zak or a clue to his whereabouts, but that hope diminished with every room he found empty. He moved up to the main level, listening. Complete silence. Maybe while he'd been in the basement, the men had left. Still, he exercised maximum caution as he searched the place, but came up empty again. Except for a piece of paper that hadn't burned all the way, stuck to the bottom of an ashtray. He could make out the letters *AA* and the numbers 0703. Flight number? Could they be that lucky? To be on the safe side, he called it in.

Frustration needled him. He wanted complete information and he wanted it now. Had Bailey not been with him, he would have nabbed one of the men and spent some time questioning him.

He could still do that. He could go back to the car and send Bailey back to the shack with it, and lie in wait here until someone else stopped by. That seemed the only way for him to move forward, as much as he disliked leaving Bailey alone even for a short time. But he didn't want her to wait for him here, for hours maybe, alone in a stolen car.

It would be great if he could make up his mind about her. Part of him wanted her with him, never leaving his sight. But he had to admit that she was safer away from what he was about to do. He would find a way to get back to the shack when he was done here.

He sneaked out the back and made his way toward the Avalon that he should probably ditch. He'd get a new car for Bailey before he went back in, something small and easy to drive, something nondescript, and tell her to stick to the side roads. She should know them—she was from around here.

But Bailey wasn't in the car.

Had she gone up to the stores? Dammit, this was not the time to window-shop. He strolled that way, scanning the people who were going about their business in the shopping plaza.

He couldn't see her.

He didn't think she would go into a shop. She was smart and perceptive, with a good head on her shoulders. She understood the precarious situation they were in. But if she wasn't shopping, where was she? His gaze settled on the fast-food restaurant in the middle of the parking lot. Maybe she'd gone to use the bathroom.

He picked a spot from where he could see most of the square and settled in to wait. Ten minutes passed. No Bailey. He started out for the restaurant, went in and sat at a booth by the bathroom doors. People came and went. Bailey wasn't one of them.

As minutes ticked by, a cold feeling pooled in the pit of his stomach. He waited until the last person he'd seen go into the ladies' room came out, and he knocked on the door. No response.

"Excuse me." He stuck his head in.

Empty.

That cold feeling solidified into a block of heavy ice, the blood running cold in his veins.

He turned and nearly bumped into a five-foot, white-haired lady with cat-eye rhinestone glasses and a disapproving look on her wrinkled face.

"Well, young man!" she said, scolding him for being where he didn't belong.

She was the least of his problems.

Bailey had been taken.

HE PASSED THE DAY IN stone-cold control. He couldn't think of Bailey, couldn't sink into despair over what they might be doing to her. He had to stay detached, focused and ready. Night came, interminably long, and his control slipped from time to time, replaced by murderous rage.

Nobody came.

Cade hid by the back door of the restaurant. This place was his only connection to the bastards, and a flimsy connection at that. He had no way of knowing how often they used the restaurant. It could be days or weeks before any of them came back here. He tried to steer clear of thoughts about what might happen to Bailey in the meanwhile.

But, of course, he couldn't. He'd seen enough, had been through enough to know. *If they touch a hair on her head, so help me God.*

HE HAD CHOSEN TO STAY with Palmer instead of going after the woman. Like he had chosen to follow Palmer back to the ruins of the house the night before instead of taking advantage of her being alone in the shack. She looked like a tasty enough morsel, but

Cade Palmer was his primary target. He was the one he couldn't afford to let out of his sight.

He could have taken the man out last night—he'd had the chance, from afar. Cleanest way, and the safest. But all of Palmer's mad comings and goings had gotten him intrigued. Maybe there was some money in whatever he was doing here.

So he'd done nothing but follow and wait all night outside the restaurant while Palmer, for whatever reason, waited within. He wasn't keen on going in after him without knowing the lay of the land. He preferred not to barge into a situation where he'd be at a disadvantage. He was as cocky as the next bastard, but smart enough to know when the odds were stacked against him. The advantage was always to those who defended any given structure, as opposed to the ones who tried to enter it.

Urban warfare 101. He'd had some practice at it.

A CAR PULLED DOWN THE alley, something old and clunky. Cade's ears perked up, and he felt that cold calm come over him that he'd often experienced before battle. His senses sharpened. The car stopped; a door opened, then closed. He moved to the peephole in the steel door and watched in the dawn's dim light as a man got out of an ancient green Chevy. Only one guy. Thirtysomething, wearing black sweatpants and a green T-shirt with combat boots. Not suspecting that his morning was about to take a turn for the worse.

He looked around carefully before he came to the door and put his key into the lock.

Cade shoved his gun into the guy's temple the second he stepped in. "Take me to your boss," he said in Arabic, in a helluva mood after the endless night he'd spent worrying about Bailey.

The guy grabbed for his own weapon. Cade ripped it from his hand, blocked a kick and shoved a well-placed elbow into the guy's chest hard enough that he doubled over. The idiot still didn't seem to comprehend the severity of his situation. "You can't do," he said between two harsh breaths, with a stupid smirk on his face. "Warrant search?" He sneered.

He wanted to see a search warrant? Did he think he was facing a cop? If Cade weren't so exhausted by the night's vigil, he would have laughed.

Instead, by way of explanation and in order to prevent wasting any more time, he slammed the butt of his gun into the man's face and didn't even wince when a bone crunched under the force. "Your boss," he said as the guy howled, fear in his eyes at last, finally catching onto the program.

And he still hesitated for another second or two before pushing his hands into the air, bright blood running down his chin. Then he turned and led Cade back to the old Chevy.

Cade checked it before getting in, scanning for weapons, which he'd have to take away. Nothing but empty soda cans on the backseat. No weapons, no documents, nothing of Bailey's, no sign that she'd been in the vehicle. Cade tied the man with his own belt, shoved him inside, then got in without taking his gun off the guy. He made one stop only—the Avalon, to grab his bag of tricks.

The ride lasted about half an hour, the man directing him to an abandoned factory building near the Philadelphia airport. And for the time being, Cade was satisfied with that, not bringing up his next question until they arrived and got out.

"Where are the kid and the woman?" He held the gun to the man's forehead, making sure he felt the reality of the barrel. At this point, he didn't care what he had to do to find the ones he sought.

Judging from the fear on the man's face, he got that.

"I don't know," he said.

"Where are the kid and the woman?" Cold rage spread through him. He wasn't going to lose them. Not this kid. Not this time. And nobody touched Bailey if they wanted to live.

"I don't know." The man fell to his knees. He was crying now, the blood on his face mixing with tears. "No kill. I don't know," he begged.

Cade got his bag of weapons and ammunition. He picked up the guy and put him in the trunk, locking him in. Then he made a single call, to the Colonel, giving his location. He'd told him about the planned attack when he'd called the day before, even though he didn't have much to go on.

"One day, the tangos said yesterday. Whatever's going down is going down today," he said grimly into the phone. Could be he had only a few hours—at best—to figure out what the plan was and stop them. And he had to save Bailey and Zak in the meantime.

Once these criminals succeeded in bringing the plane down, they would have no need for hostages. Their goal achieved, they would want to clear out fast. If they didn't succeed, Bailey and Zak would be on hand for revenge. Either way, there was little time left.

"By the way, there is no American Airlines flight number 0703 out of Philadelphia, or anyplace else. Aviation security decided to put the airport under lockdown until further notice, anyway. Other American Airlines hubs are under heightened security all around the country," the Colonel told him.

He sure hoped that would be enough. "They should pay special attention to flights to Africa." As long as he wasn't mistaken about the men's accents. And then it popped into his mind. "Air Africana?"

"That would be AFR."

"Could be. I don't know. The paper I found was half burned."

"Could be they weren't using official aviation codes for their communications. Maybe it's their own code. I'll get someone on that and have Air Africana checked. You stay put, and don't do anything crazy. How bad is it?"

"Undetermined number of tangos inside," he reported. "They have two hostages. I have one of the tangos disabled in the trunk of an old Chevy up front."

"Reinforcements are coming. I repeat, stay put. That's an order." The Colonel's voice was as stark as he'd ever heard it. "You can't make any mistakes here, Cade. The FBI still wants your head on a stick."

"Yes, sir." He closed his phone, grabbed his bag

of tricks and took off toward the old factory, running along the fence, keeping low to the ground.

SHE WOULDN'T HAVE THOUGHT this much pain was possible. Bailey rested her back against the cool wall of the small room in the basement where they had brought her after yet another round of "questioning." Her clothes were covered with blood and sweat.

But the worst wasn't what they had done to her. The worst was knowing that they had probably done the same to Zak. They wouldn't care that he was just a kid. Some of the monsters who had worked her over weren't much older than he was.

"Where is the electromagnetic weapon?" "What were you doing at the restaurant?" "Who do you work for?" The questions had been endless.

Pretending that she'd only gone to see if the place was opening had been useless. There was no point denying her identity. They knew who she was. They had a picture of her, taken in front of the garden center where she worked. It had been taken a week ago, as she was getting into her car after her shift. Her skin crawled with the thought that she'd been watched by these creeps.

No use in protesting her innocence, either. They had found her gun. The gun she hadn't even been able to pull before she was so effortlessly captured. She was spitting mad at herself for that. She had failed Cade and failed herself—but what hurt the most was that she had failed Zak.

She'd thought she was so tough, knowing how

to use a gun, searching for her nephew and going after Cade, assuming she could help. She was nothing but easy prey.

The room was empty, just bare cement walls, a steel door, a bare lightbulb hanging from the ceiling and some kind of vent with a grating over it. It was close to the floor and too small to fit through, even if she could get the grating off with her hands tied behind her back.

That should be her first priority—her hands. Her arms were going numb from the way her shoulders had been twisted back. She rolled up into a ball and squeezed her legs through the loop of her arms. Then she could finally roll her shoulders to get some blood circulating. Better.

She tried the door. Locked, of course. Looked at the lightbulb. Too high to reach. Although even if she could have reached it, gotten it out and broken it, she might still not have been able to cut the hard plastic cuff they'd tied her with.

She fought not to give in to desperation. If there was nothing she could do now, she would wait until they came for her again. With her hands in front of her, she'd have a better chance. All she needed was one lucky break, to be able to grab a gun. And then she could go find Zak.

He could be as close as the next room and she wouldn't know it. That gave her an idea. She moved to the vent on the wall and pressed her mouth against it. "Zak?" she whispered. "Zak?"

No response came.

But she could see light at the other end of the duct, which was short, leading to another room close by. Maybe she could stick her head in and see what was there. She ran her hand over the dried paint that clogged the slight crack between the vent cover and the wall, then pushed a fingernail in and tried to pry the damn thing loose.

Other than nearly ripping her nail off, nothing happened. She tried again. This time she felt a slight movement. She began to pull harder.

When the cover was finally off, she realized that the duct between the rooms was much larger than the metal grating that closed it off. A single line of bricks narrowed it down around the edges. She began to work on those. When it was clear that the mortar wouldn't give under her hands, she lay on her side and kicked at the bricks.

She could have shouted in triumph when the first brick moved. But she didn't stop to celebrate. She got it out and moved on to work on the next, and the next.

When the duct was unblocked at last, she wiggled through, headfirst. She figured if someone was in the other room, they would have already responded to all the noise she'd made.

The room was empty and smaller than her own. And the door was open. That was where the light had come from. The main area of the basement spread before her, filled with pipes and heaters and all manner of industrial equipment which she couldn't have identified if her life depended on it. Nor did she have to. All she had to do was to find Zak and then get out of here.

A path led to a stairway straight ahead, but she didn't want to leave the basement until she'd searched it fully. She hustled forward with her feet tied together, her shuffling footsteps echoing in the empty space, aware that they could be back for her at any moment. She had to be quick and stay out of sight. No unnecessary heroics, either. She would be no use to Zak dead.

THE PLACE WAS CRAWLING with tangos. Cade could hear several of them talking behind the front entry. All other entries were security-grade steel. Nothing but an explosion could have gotten him in, which he could have provided, but if the tangos thought they were under attack, they might kill Zak and Bailey outright. *If* they were even in the building. That he didn't know for sure was driving him crazy.

From what he'd seen so far—reinforced doors and plenty of men on guard duty—all signs pointed to the abandoned factory being tango headquarters. If they thought this was where they were the safest, it made sense that they would bring Zak and Bailey here.

He stole around the whole building and eyed the first-floor windows. The fact that they were at least eight feet off the ground wasn't much of an obstacle to him. The windows' thick iron bars were, however. Same with the smaller basement windows at ground level. But he did find one in the back that was broken. He got down onto his stomach to look in through the bars. He couldn't see anything but machinery in there.

He had to get inside. He stood. His only chance

was through the front door. But he wouldn't make it through with the arsenal he carried. He opened the bag and pulled out a ratty old watch, then searched around the bottom and found a thin, naked blade. He pressed that into the bottom of his shoe. He set his cell phone to transmit a locator signal and then stashed it in the bag's hidden pocket. Even if someone found his bag and took it away, the cell would still transmit the location to the Colonel in case they had trouble finding the place. The building was out in the middle of an abandoned industrial area, not a street sign in sight. He'd only been able to give an approximate location when they'd talked.

He checked his gun in the back of his waistband. If he went completely unarmed, they'd be suspicious.

He was about to shove his bag through the bars when his phone buzzed. The Colonel.

"Good. You're staying put," the man said. "A team will be there in an hour, tops. I'm on my way to JFK. There was an Air Africana flight this morning. The number you had was the departure time. Unfortunately, it took off half an hour ago. The plane is in the air."

Cade swore. The Colonel didn't tolerate a foul mouth. But for once, he didn't chastise him.

"It gets worse. The Sub-Saharan Security Council is on board. If something happens to them, all hell is going to break lose in the Sudan."

Joey Tanner was Cade's first thought, and the woman he'd gone there to save. No way he could have reached her yet.

Cade hesitated only a second. "Tanner is in the Sudan, sir."

"He's on vacation. Let's focus on the trouble we have on hand here."

He didn't contradict the Colonel. After a moment, he could hear a deep breath being drawn on the other end. "In the Sudan where?"

"Some refugee camp."

"*You* stay put," the Colonel said.

As he hung up, Cade knew that the Colonel was getting back on the phone, ordering help for Tanner. A plane would show up, or a UN convoy would be diverted. And when Tanner got back, he'd get a chewing out he wouldn't soon forget.

Cade put the phone back into the bag, dropping it to the floor inside. When he heard no further sound, he got up and ran around the building to the front.

He didn't go in with guns blazing. He didn't want to be shot before he had a chance to put his plan in motion. That was the trick, the most dangerous part of his dangerous plan. But he had no other choice and time was of the essence. He held his weapon in hand as he pushed the heavy front door in. A half dozen rifles were pointed at his head instantly. Cade swore, then made a show of fighting with himself about whether or not to give up. After a tense moment, he dropped his gun.

A rifle butt slammed into his side, then another one into his face. He went down, curled up to protect his vital organs and waited for them to be done with the introductory beating before they would take him inside.

"What are you doing?" someone shouted in Arabic over the melee.

The kicking stopped. The men were talking over each other, offering explanations about how he'd shown up.

"Who are you?" The man came closer and, as a way of greeting, kicked Cade in the face. Wasn't too bad. Unlike the others, who had military boots on, this guy wore sandals.

Cade spit blood from his mouth. "I'm looking for a woman and a boy. I'll pay for them." He spoke in English. If they thought he was just a boyfriend, they'd be less vigilant than if they thought him some sort of military man or law enforcement.

"I don't have time for this. Take him downstairs," the man said to the others in Arabic.

Someone produced a length of plastic rope, and they tied his hands. Two men pulled him up, roughly, and marched him down the corridor, pointing their rifles at his head. There were only six of them. There was a ninety-nine percent probability that he could take them out without suffering serious damage himself. But since there were other lives at stake, he wasn't willing to take that one percent chance. Instead, he bided his time as they shoved him through the door and down a set of stairs.

Bingo. His weapons were somewhere down here. Hopefully, they wouldn't tumble right over them. But the tangos shoved him along one of the many paths that zigzagged through the maze of machinery, never going anywhere near the outer walls.

He kept an eye out for Bailey or Zak, but saw no sign of either. He was led to a cell-like room. One of the men hit him in the side of the head, hard. He went down, figuring that was what they wanted. No point in showing his strength. They tied his feet together and locked him in.

He didn't even wait a full minute before starting to work on getting out. The blade in the bottom of his shoe was easy enough to reach. He freed his hands first, then his feet. He popped the back off his watch and took out his picks. He was through the door in seconds.

He found the quickest way to the outer wall and moved to the back, keeping an eye out for his bag. Not there.

What the hell?

He could have really used that damn thing. His cell phone, the machine gun, the two hand grenades. He found the broken window and jumped up to look out, confirming that this was the right one. Sure was. His bag had disappeared. No time to cry over it. He moved on silently. He could see a few doors down here that probably led to closed-off areas like the one he'd been kept in. Weapons or no weapons, he had to find Bailey and Zak.

He tapped on the first door. No sound. Then again, if anyone was in there, he or she could be unconscious, or gagged. He used his picks to get in. Nobody. He went to the next door. Same result.

He was about to move on when an acrid smell hit his nose. He straightened and smelled the air. Smoke, somewhere in the far corner. Fire? Something cold slithered across his skin. He hated fire. Smoke seeped into you and stayed with you forever.

Could be just some machinery breaking down. But what would be running in an abandoned building, and why? He moved to investigate, but before he could go around a giant industrial transformer, the barrel of a machine gun popped out, aimed straight at him.

A guard must have been posted down here. When he hadn't seen anyone outside his cell, he'd thought he was in the clear. Nobody had come down while he searched—he would have heard the door or steps on the stairs. He'd been listening for that. Damn.

He was in a narrow aisle with no place to go. He was too far away to grab for the barrel of the weapon, but close enough that if whoever held the semiautomatic squeezed off a barrage of bullets, he couldn't miss.

"Stop!"

"Bailey?" His knees went weak with relief. Damn funny thing to happen in the middle of a mission. Good thing he was retired.

"Cade?" Her head popped out.

All weakness disappeared, and the urge to kill swept over him. Her beautiful face was bruised; smudges of blood were on her lips. Whoever was responsible for this was a dead man.

Deep breath. She was alive. That was the most important thing. They had worked her over, but she was alive. Nothing else was going to happen to her. He could guarantee that—even if he had to rip apart the sons of bitches with his own hands. He tamped down his anger, and when he could speak without growling, he said, "You okay?"

She trembled a little, pressed her lips together and immediately winced. Then she lowered the gun and stepped into his arms. "Oh, God, Cade."

"Hey, you're gonna be fine. I'm taking you out of this place." He didn't dare hold her too tight, unsure how bad her injuries might be. She was back in his arms. He'd found her. The powerful emotions that swirled through him caught him off guard. He had to bury them away and focus on getting out. For now. "Did you find Zak?"

She pulled away, worry taking over her momentarily relieved expression. "Not yet. He's not in the basement. But I found this." She smiled and pulled up the gun again. "And a knife, and a whole bunch of other stuff I have no idea what to do with."

She had his bag. They had everything. He kissed her without even thinking about it. Just a quick light brush of his lips against hers. He had the pleasure of watching her eyes fill with surprise.

That acrid smell reached him again, stronger this time. He glanced around but couldn't yet see the smoke anywhere. Not that it meant much. He'd seen places go from smoky to completely engulfed in flames in under ten minutes. Waiting around for reinforcements was now unequivocally ruled out. Not that that option had ever played heavily into his plans.

"We have to get out. I think there's a fire somewhere down here."

She drew herself straight, resting the butt of the machine gun against her hip in some "Lara Croft, Tomb Raider" pose, as her battered lips widened into a brilliant smile.

"I know. I started it," she said.

Chapter Ten

"Why?" The look on his face made it clear that he failed to recognize her brilliance. He looked dark and more than a little angry.

Men.

"I have to get them out of this place so I can go up and look for Zak." She was pretty sure that the universe favored her plan and that was why it sent Cade and his bag of weapons to help. She didn't think it would be any use pointing that out to him. With the cold light in his eyes and the tight expression on his face, he didn't look like he was completely in tune with the universe at this moment.

"How many people have you seen?" He took his attention from her at last and was scanning the place as if he were trying to memorize it.

"About a dozen." *Please, please dear God, don't let there be more.* A dozen men were enough to bury the two of them ten times over.

"I figure there are at least double," he said, nixing her hopes just like that. Where was *his* positive thinking? "What do you know about the floors above?" he asked.

"I've only been to the first floor." Not the land of happy memories, for sure. The interrogation chamber was up there. "Other than the lobby, it's all giant rooms with rows of workstations and one small office in the back."

He moved toward the stairs, pulling her behind him. "They hurt you bad?" He wouldn't look at her.

"What are you talking about?" She could joke now that he was here. "Those weasel bastards breaking me? Never."

He squeezed her hand but kept on moving. His chest expanded with a deep breath. She noticed because she'd been staring at his wide shoulders that rose like a shield in front of her.

He let go of her hand when they reached the stairs, motioned her to stay silent and went first, machine gun drawn. She kept her own weapon at the ready, appreciating that he hadn't asked her to stay behind. Her nephew was up there. At least she hoped he was.

"If anything goes wrong…" The words slipped from her lips unbidden. Lord, what was wrong with her? Where was *her* positive thinking?

He halted and turned back. "Nothing's going to go wrong." And then he drew her into his arms.

She didn't protest when he dipped his head to hers and their lips met in a quick kiss that, despite its brevity, was sure potent enough.

She felt her body relax a little and a small smile spread on her face as he pulled back, his caramel eyes full with emotion. "Thank you for coming after me. I'm really glad that you're here."

He held her gaze for a long moment before he nodded. "Let's find Zak."

They didn't stop again until they were at the top of the stairs. He tried the door. Locked. He took off his watch, flipped it over and shook out a couple of picks that were about as long as a needle, flexible enough to be bent at any angle he needed. The man came prepared.

Before she had a chance to comment, however, he'd mastered the lock and was already checking outside.

"All clear." His voice was barely audible.

She stepped out into the empty hallway after him. He moved silently and she did her best to copy him. She didn't exactly succeed, but she was good enough that nobody would hear her coming from a mile away.

They could hear men talking in the front. Cade moved toward the back, checking every room systematically as he went. The building wasn't huge—it had a footprint of maybe ten thousand square feet and about a dozen floors. They swept through the ground floor pretty fast, then circled back to the bank of elevators but didn't take one. Instead, they crept up the staircase.

The next floor was pretty much the same as the one below—large, open work spaces with a few offices along the walls. The search didn't take long. Unfortunately, they were out in the open when the elevator suddenly dinged and the doors opened.

The two camouflage-clad men inside opened fire

immediately. Cade shoved her down behind him and returned fire, hitting both men. The gunshots echoed in the cavernous room, deafening.

Okay, so the stealth part of the mission was over. Everyone in the building would now know that something was up.

Bailey stared at the two dead men. Cade grabbed her hand and dragged her toward the stairs. "Let's go."

They ran into another group at the top of the stairs. Four this time. She tried to help, unsure if she hit any of them with the bullets she managed to squeeze off. But they all went down and neither Cade nor she was injured. It all seemed surreal, like one of Zak's video games she'd tried at the beginning of summer in the hopes that if they did things together, he might open up to her a little. War of the Brechinans II.

But this was the real thing.

When they rushed by the dead bodies, she tried not to look at them this time.

The hallway on the next floor was empty. It had the same setup as the others.

"Want to split up?" she asked. If Zak was here, he'd be in one of the offices that lined the outer walls. They could go twice as fast if they went in opposite directions. The central area of the floor was empty, at least on their side. In the middle, the main supporting walls of the building divided the space into four quarters.

Cade hesitated. "If you need me, fire off a shot." He ran off to the left.

She went right, reconsidering her bravado as soon as he was out of sight. But she pushed on. His vote of confidence was empowering. He thought she could handle herself. She appreciated that.

None of the offices were locked, because there was nothing in there to protect. They were stripped bare.

She checked door after door and prayed for a knob that wouldn't turn under her hand, a locked room that might hold Zak. No such luck. She met up with Cade a few minutes later.

"Next floor," he said.

Suddenly they could hear men near the stairs, shouting.

She glanced around, looking out the nearest window. "Fire escape?"

He flashed her a wide grin and started running toward it.

She went after him, watching as he easily pushed open a metal window that had looked rusted shut. Some dirt smudged his face. His entire being was focused, his gun ready, his shoulders rising like a shield in front of her once again.

If I ever do come to believe in love, this would be the man.

The thought came out of left field and begged further analysis, but they were climbing up a rusty fire escape the next second. Smoke drifted from a basement window way below them. Her muscles clenched as she choked back a cough. But Cade didn't let her fall behind. He reached for her hand and pulled her after him.

When they reached the next level, he took off his watch again, popped the back and used its supersharp edge to cut a small hole in the glass. Then he reached in to turn the lock.

"Where do you get stuff like that?" She thumped softly to the floor next to him.

"An old job," was all he said.

"And here I thought you were a retired programmer," she joked.

He gave her a practiced, bland smile. "I used to design databases for a bank in Delaware."

"Right, and I'm Tinker Bell." She rolled her eyes.

There were no offices on their end of this floor. They crept forward to check out the other side of the divider walls in the middle. "Given the circumstances, don't you think I should know a little more about you?" Mostly, she needed a distraction. She was running on pure adrenaline, with little to hold her up beyond that.

"All you need to know is that you're crazy about me." His eyes glinted dangerously, but a smile hovered on his lips.

"I don't think so."

"You're full of pixie dust, Tinker Bell." He let loose a full-powered grin then. "You admitted the first week I moved in that I rock your world. No sense going into denial now."

"I said you're as hardheaded as a rock," she responded. They'd had that conversation when he had backed over her favorite garden flag.

"You gonna pick at technicalities at a moment like this?" He was moving forward.

Truth was, she really *was* starting to care about

him, and it wasn't just the way he made her feel every time their lips touched. The thought was not only annoying, it was also untimely and inconvenient. They reached the back wall, and the dozen offices that lined it, and split up. This time she actually welcomed the space between them.

"Do you think Zak might not even be here?" she asked when they met up again.

"It's possible, but I'm betting that he is."

"Why?"

"Instinct," he said.

So this was what it came down to. Trusting the instincts of a man she barely knew, heading into mortal danger with him. Except that Cade wasn't just any man. The more time she spent with him, the more she realized his strength, his honor, his incredible courage—some of which was somehow rubbing off on her. On her own, she would have never attempted any of this.

"Hey." He caught her gaze. "I'm not leaving here without him. Or without you."

A door banged open across the floor before she could respond. People started shouting.

They kept low and kept moving, always making sure there was a dividing wall between them and the men. When they reached the window where they'd come in, they exited silently and moved up to the next level.

"How many more?" she asked as she looked up.

"Six," he said.

The smoke coming from the basement was definitely getting thicker. Looked like the first-floor windows were leaking smoke, too. She moved faster.

The next three floors clearly belonged to production. The floor above those, however, held rows and rows of offices and took three times as long to search through, though they saw no men there.

The next floor was positively crawling with people. Luckily for them, most were on their way down to escape the fire. Only a few remained, standing guard, scattered through the space.

Bailey and Cade managed to avoid them while searching most of the floor before their luck finally ran out. As they turned the next corner, a man was running toward them. Surprise flashed across the guy's face, his mouth opening. Whatever he was about to shout didn't amount to more than a stifled groan, however.

She barely saw Cade's hand move. She would have thought it was a trick of her eyes if it weren't for the knife buried deep in the man's chest. He fell to the floor, but neither he nor his rifle made much noise on the industrial carpet.

Cade reached him first, pulled his knife out, wiped it on the man's shirt, then stepped over him. She kept her gaze on Cade and jumped over the body, trying to avoid contact. And then she couldn't believe she'd done it—just jumped right on over a dead man. And had to wonder if her life would ever be the same again.

But to have a life of any kind required that they got out of here alive.

"Stick as close to me as you can," Cade said.

She had no inclination to argue. Her only hope was that the extra security up here might mean that they did have Zak stashed nearby.

The first office Cade pushed into held only two armed men. He took them out with a minimum of firepower, but they could hear others reacting, running toward them. There was no place to hide. He hugged the wall on one side of the door, and she went to the other side.

He yanked her over to him in the last second. "We'd cut each other down in the cross fire."

"Of course," she mumbled, embarrassed that she hadn't thought of that. Good thing one of them had experience.

As soon as the first terrorists came through, they fired at will. Cade killed two more when he stepped out from cover. The area outside the office was temporarily clear.

They checked the rest of the offices but found no sign of Zak. As they rushed back to the fire escape, black smoke rose outside the window like a wall, blocking their sight completely.

She could feel the heat of it even through the glass. "I don't think we should go out in that."

"Elevators." Cade was running that way even as he said the word. He pushed the button. Nothing happened. The elevators probably went to the nearest floor and opened, then shut down, the result of an emergency system. The freight elevators at the garden center were like that, a feature always emphasized at their biannual workplace-safety workshop.

"Looks like the staircase is our only option." He was pulling a hand grenade from his back pocket as he moved toward the staircase door. He opened it and took a step forward until he could look down. He pulled the tab on the grenade and let it go while she contemplated whether to have a stroke or a heart attack.

"Back, get back!" He pushed her out of the staircase and closed the door behind them, stepping to the side and pulling her down with him. "Can't get out that way, anyway, and I don't want anyone coming up from the lower floors, getting behind our backs." He put his arms around her.

The explosion several floors below them was strong enough to slam the door open, dust and smoke billowing all the way up to their level.

"Hold your shirt in front of your nose." He charged into the staircase without waiting for the air to settle.

She could see little as he moved in front of her. As long as he was there, she told herself, she had hope—even if they were about to search the last floor and still no sign of Zak.

The building was on fire, the elevators didn't work, the staircase had blown up, the fire escape was smothered in smoke and impassable. She really could have used a sign from the universe that everything was going to turn out just fine.

But when they rushed up the stairs and opened the door to the top floor, they found themselves staring into the face of hell.

The universe wanted her dead.

HE SHOULD HAVE TAKEN her out of here, taken her to safety before he came back for Zak, Cade thought, knowing that she wouldn't have stood for that, not for a second. Still, he should have found a way to avoid bringing her into this. Damn, he was a soldier. He must have known at least two dozen ways to restrain and immobilize any man or woman.

A small army occupied the top floor.

Running back to the staircase wasn't an option. One, it was now severely damaged. Two, if Zak were in the building, he'd be up here. They had searched every other place. Luckily, the building was made of steel and cement, with no furniture or curtains that easily caught on fire, as there would have been in a residential structure. And the lower floors, with their open spaces, had been easy and quick to search.

He dashed to the right, out of sight, dragging Bailey after him, hoping no one caught the movement. None of the men rushing down the hall were looking their way.

But someone must have seen them, because a shout rang out and boots thudded on the floor, coming toward them.

"Go! Go! Go!" He ducked into the maze of cubicles.

As long as they kept down, they'd be hard to spot. They moved forward swiftly, playing hide-and-seek for many long minutes. But he knew they didn't have much time left. The men who hunted them must have realized that the fire was a serious threat, because they called to each other with increasing urgency.

Then someone quieted them, and Cade popped up

because he needed to know how many men were up here and where they were located.

But as soon as he stuck his head out, he was greeted by a barrage of bullets. And cubicle walls weren't bulletproof—far from it.

He swore under his breath as he dashed to the left, then to the right, to the right again, Bailey close behind him. He could hear her breathing hard. They'd been rushing through the floors, searching as fast as they could, stopping only when it was absolutely necessary to keep from being discovered. She wasn't a trained soldier. She was winded, and he knew it wasn't going to work like this. He had to go faster and quieter.

He stopped when he got to a metal supply cabinet, opened the door and mouthed, "In there."

Her eyes widened. She shook her head.

He raised his eyebrows. They didn't have time to argue. She must have understood that because after giving him the evil eye, she slipped in to crouch on the bottom shelf.

He knew what he had to do, but he had trouble leaving her. He was certifiable. As if to prove that, he reached into his pocket and held out his last hand grenade.

Her face said it all. "Are you crazy?" she whispered.

Yeah, he was. Crazy worried about her. He closed the door, leaving an inch or so for air, before he quietly rolled a chair in front of it and moved on. He used the discipline he'd gained over nearly twenty years of active duty to put Bailey from his mind and assess the situation around them.

He couldn't face all the men at once, but he had a fair chance if he went after them one by one. He stopped to listen and heard a sound on the other side of the cubicle wall to his right. Whoever it was, he was moving west. Cade stole east to get behind him and used his knife. The guy went down quietly. Cade made it to his side in time to assure that his AK-47 didn't clang against the desk.

He could smell smoke up here now, too. Time to get out of this death trap. He heard another noise to his right and crept toward it. Two men. Damn. He was good with the knife, but not that good. Explosives had been his specialty. But his C4 had gone up with his house.

And blowing up the building you were in was never a good idea, anyway. At least, that was what his SDDU trainer had told him way back when. So he opened fire on the men, then ran like hell before their buddies could get there to see what was going on.

The next guy he heard, he shot straight through the gray, cloth-covered cubicle wall. Hell, the cat was out of the bag now, anyway—they all knew that someone was up here. Better that they came after him than found Bailey.

He moved forward. It was a search-and-destroy mission, clear and simple. His senses were sharp, his mind focused. He didn't think of the men he took down—all he thought of was finishing the job.

Clearing the maze of cubicles took him less than ten minutes. He went back for Bailey.

She was no longer in the supply cabinet. Had she gone off to look for Zak?

If there were no other complications, if she already had Zak, there was a slim chance that they could make it to the roof and he could call the Colonel for a chopper before the flames and the smoke made a helicopter's landing impossible. On second thought, he'd make that call now, just to be sure. Cade hung up before the Colonel started shouting.

He had smoke in his nose now, good and deep, the acrid smell infiltrating his brain. He could smell and see that other fire, four months ago. Pachi. He shut the images down. Couldn't go there. Wouldn't go there. He couldn't let doubt in, nor his old rage, nor fear—not if he wanted to succeed. He would find Bailey. And if any tango harmed as much as a hair on her head, he would rip the bastard's heart out with his bare hands.

He moved on to another row of offices. The first was empty. The second was, too. He was running for time now. Empty, empty, empty. Until the very last one.

A regal-looking man in a white caftan sat, flanked by two bodyguards whose rifles were aimed at Bailey's chest. He briefly registered the large walk-in safe in the back. There were no other men, and no way out.

The boss had a weapon, too—a funky-looking handgun pressed tight against the back of Bailey's head.

Everyone had their fingers on the triggers, everyone watching to see what move he might make, nobody wanting to catch the first bullet.

Tension was visible on the men's faces, except for

the boss. He looked a little like Ruvaraj on the day when Cade, based on a tip from Pachaimani, had finally busted up a major money transfer he was completing for a new terrorist group. This man, like Ruvaraj, had a solemn look to him. He thought himself a called man, a holy man, believing that nothing and no one could come between him and his purpose.

He didn't know Cade.

Images of that last fight in the deepest hell of Indonesia flickered in his brain, and he let them come, let them give him strength. He had led the charge on Ruvaraj's compound. But it hadn't been a surprise attack. He'd been betrayed by one of his assets—Smith, a mercenary turned businessman. Smith had been feeding the U.S. information for years. They hadn't known that he was playing both sides.

The mighty Ruvaraj died that day, as Cade had promised Pachaimani. And Pachaimani already had his sister, hidden under his tiny bed right in the compound. Cade had promised to take them out to safety once the place was cleared. But he couldn't keep that part of his promise. Before he could get Pachaimani out, Cade was mowed down and caught some shrapnel in his lungs, courtesy of Smith. His team had barely been able to keep him alive long enough to get him out of there.

But this wasn't going to end like that.

The bastards had Bailey. But he had a plan.

Chapter Eleven

Bailey watched with wide-eyed shock as Cade dropped his weapon and stepped away from it.

Her hopes crashed to the floor along with his semi-automatic. Sweat rolled down her face. She gasped for air that was growing hotter and hotter, choking on smoke and on her own fear as panic squeezed her lungs.

The two guards moved to either side of Cade, anger on their faces. But in their stiff movements, she recognized some of the fear she felt. They knew the building was burning.

"The authorities know where you are and what you are up to. You have three hostages," Cade said. "You need us all alive."

The man in white examined Cade first, then Bailey. "Why are you here?"

"For Zak," Bailey said. "Please. He's just a kid." She coughed as smoke scratched her throat. "We have to get out of here."

"He will be dealt with." The man spit the words out, his tone laden with anger.

Will? That meant he was still alive. Oh, thank God. "Is he here?"

The man pushed his gun harder into her skin, hate burning in his eyes.

"The FBI knows about your plans. They are on their way." Cade lurched forward, but the two guards yanked him back.

The man only sneered. "Too late. My sons already left."

"They know about Air Africana. They are turning the plane around." Cade was only half bluffing. The Colonel had said the plane was in the air already by the time they figured out what was going on. But information would have been radioed to the pilot immediately, and emergency measures had likely been taken. "This building is on fire. There's no way down. The staircase is out."

She didn't know if he was scaring them or not, but he was sure scaring her. She really, really hoped he had some kind of a backup plan. Especially since the fire was so close now that the building was creaking, popping and groaning, making it hard to hear what anybody said.

"Nobody has to die." Cade wouldn't give up. "We can all go to the roof and call for a rescue helicopter. You get the boy and we all go."

"Our sacrifice will make a difference. We die as heroes. We will die praying. Pray with us." The leader stepped back from her. "Whatever needs to happen will happen."

But his idea about what needed to happen was

apparently different from Cade's. The second that gun was taken off her, Cade broke free of the guards and leaped into the air, his boots connecting with the guards' rifles. Before they could recapture their weapons, he had killed them both with his bare hands.

Three days ago, she would have thrown up at the sight of such violence. Now she was diving for one of the AK-47s. A bullet pinged by her ear. She whirled to shove the gun in the boss's face without hesitation before he could get another shot off. "Where is my nephew? Where is Zak?"

The smoke was thickest around the door to the staircase, spreading through the floor. It hovered along the ceiling.

Desperation gave her strength. "Where—is—Zak?" she asked as Cade collected his own gun and the other AK-47. "If you don't tell me where my nephew is, I'm going to shoot you, so help me God."

Cade was approaching to back her up.

A strange thing happened then. An odd expression slid over the man's face. He held her gaze, but the light had gone out of his eyes and a stillness came over him. Then, with a lightning-quick move, he put his hands over Bailey's, and before she could do anything, he squeezed the trigger.

As if in a nightmare, she saw the man fall. Blood was everywhere. Then she was pressed against Cade's chest. She needed the comfort of his strong arms like she'd never needed it before, but they had no time.

"How will we find Zak?" She pulled away, looking at the bodies of the two guards on the floor. No one was alive to tell them where Zak was.

As much as she had wanted to find the kid here, now she was beginning to hope that they were wrong about him being in the building. He would be safer just about anywhere else. The chances of them making it out of here alive were getting slimmer by the second.

Cade let go of her and walked to the giant safe in the back.

She hadn't thought of that. She hadn't thought of much but how to survive from one minute to the next. She stared at the keypad in the middle of the safe.

Cade banged the butt of the AK-47 against the steel door. "Zak?"

She began shouting, too, slamming her bare fists against the barrier. "Zak? Are you in there?" She prayed for an answer while Cade was examining the keypad.

"Can you open it? Is there a way to override it?" She coughed. The smoke was becoming thicker and thicker.

"I know people who could, but there's no way to get them here in time." He banged with the rifle again.

She coughed so hard that she doubled over and slid to the floor, her lungs burning. Cade crouched to the same level. "It's better to stay down." He put a hand on her shoulder. He searched her face and she knew that he was considering grabbing her and taking her out. But when he opened his mouth, he said, "Where is the grenade I gave you?"

She scrambled toward one of the guards and tried

not to look at all the blood as she reached into the dead man's pocket. "Here."

Cade tapped the safe door again. "If you're in there, stand back." He pulled the pin, leaned the grenade against the bottom of the door and grabbed her, diving for cover with her in his arms, straight through the office door, rolling to the side.

Bang!

Debris and dust flew by them, pouring out of the safe. She followed him in without hesitation, blindly. And as the air somewhat cleared, she could see the inside of the safe at last, beyond the violently twisted door.

A still form lay on the floor, tied and gagged.

"Zak?" She rushed forward, but Cade was bringing him out already, cutting his ropes.

"Can you walk? Keep low." He went down, pulling both Bailey and Zak with him.

The kid was clearly rattled, his red-rimmed eyes widening as he looked at her. "Aunt Bailey?" He coughed as smoke entered his lungs. "I'm so sorry. I heard the FBI talking to Dad about your house. I only did this to get back at those men. I didn't realize… After the FBI, I got in touch with them and told them it was all a joke, that it was all off. I never thought they'd try to hurt you. But they found out where I was and they—"

"You had something to do with these men?" She was too stunned to process the implications. "What were you thinking, Zak?" She wanted to wring the kid's neck.

They rushed after Cade to the staircase, into the smoke and heat, which was a hundred times worse behind the staircase door.

"I've been trying to hack into odd systems, looking for links to terrorists. I just wanted to find them, then tell the CIA."

"Are you crazy?" She grabbed his wrist and dragged him after her.

"Up, up, up," Cade called back.

Hell burned below them. They didn't need too much encouragement.

"I found some e-mails and stuff. I wasn't sure. There was a lot of coded stuff I didn't get. I figured if I set a trap—"

"God, this can't be true. You know how much trouble you are in? You know that you almost got us killed?"

Cade broke open the metal door to the roof. Then they were outside, where the air was a little more breathable. But the advantage was only marginal and temporary at best. The wind whipped around the black smoke that drifted up the sides of the building, flames licking the edge of the roof.

Zak's eyes were bright red. "I never meant for any of this to happen. That plane went down and I... It seemed like the perfect trap to set."

"I'm going to tell your father to send you to military school. And this guy here—" she nodded toward Cade "—is going to help to get you in."

"I'm sorry, Aunt Bailey."

I could strangle this kid. But she really wanted to

hug him for all she was worth, and keep on hugging him forever. "We'll discuss this later."

"Do you think Dad will be mad?"

Livid. But she couldn't think about that now. There was no rescue chopper in the air and no time to call one.

No way down.

Sirens blared all around; she could see fire trucks and police, tons of them. But no ladder could reach all the way up here.

She dragged her nephew to her at last and wrapped her arms around him tight. "Oh, Zak. You should have never gotten involved with this. But whatever you did, I'm always going to love you."

"I'm sorry, Aunt Bailey. I'm so sorry."

She didn't get to reassure him that it didn't matter now. A chopper drowned out her voice.

"Come on, guys," Cade said. He ran toward the middle of the roof, where it was free of vent stacks.

Hope leaped in her heart. She dragged Zak behind her. But instead of setting down, the chopper hovered. "What's wrong?"

Cade surveyed the roof, a tight look coming over his face. "Not enough clearance."

Then the chopper's door opened, and a guy appeared. A rope ladder unfurled next, swinging wildly in the wind. But Cade caught it.

The whole idea seemed insane. She didn't have time to panic. She pushed the boy toward Cade. "Take Zak first," she said.

"Can you take him?" asked Cade.

"Are you crazy?" He wanted them both safe, and while she appreciated that, she also knew that she didn't have the necessary strength to get Zak into the chopper.

"I'm coming back." Cade stepped up on the bottom rung, showed Zak where to put his feet, then put his free arm around the boy and held him tight. Then he signaled to the pilot.

For a moment, before the chopper pulled up, Cade looked straight into her eyes. "I'll be back for you, I swear. Do you trust me?"

"With all my heart," she shouted over the ungodly noise as the chopper rose up and banked to the left.

Then she was alone on the top of a burning roof. The flames had spread to the tarp on the back corner of the building, moving closer and closer to her. She pulled her shirt up and covered her nose with it. She was dizzy, her lungs burning from smoke inhalation. She sat down, pulled her legs up and rested her forehead on her knees.

No matter what happened to her, Zak and Cade were going to be safe. She kept her focus on that.

"WHAT DO YOU MEAN the chopper can't go back?" Cade shouted, wishing to hell that he hadn't left his weapons on the roof.

The FBI boneheads weren't listening to him, and the Colonel was on his way to JFK airport to wait for the plane which was turning around. The Colonel had called to check in and see how things were going on Cade's end just after the chopper had set down.

Since the Sub-Saharan Security Council was on

board, Air Africana had requested and received several air marshals for the flight. They successfully disarmed the terrorists once information had been passed along to the cockpit. All was well, all passengers safe.

But Bailey was dying on the roof.

"The updraft from the hot air is too much. You barely made it out. As bad as it is now, it would take down the chopper. Look, there's zero visibility up there."

"I know there's zero damn visibility. There is a woman up there." He climbed right into the man's face. "Do you understand that?"

DAMN AUTHORITIES WERE here. FBI. Cops. Firemen. He had hoped the fire would take care of Palmer for him, but that hadn't happened. Which meant he had to take matters into his own hands. He was done delaying. Whatever Palmer was involved in was just getting messier and messier. If it had to do with money, he'd figure that out later and see if anything could be salvaged. He was ready to make his move. Chaos reigned around the fire, and Palmer was going to play into his hands.

"I'M SORRY. LOOK," the agent was saying.

But Cade wasn't in the mood to look. He shoved the guy aside and headed to the fire truck nearest the building. Water splattered back and down from the burning walls as men in yellow suits and oxygen masks fought to control the blaze.

He went to the east side, where the fire hadn't

taken over yet. Only one guy was assessing the situation there. "I need your suit and tank," he said.

"Get back, sir. You need to get out of the way."

"I'm sorry. I don't have time to explain." He knocked the guy out—he hated doing it, but not as much as he would have hated losing Bailey. That wasn't an option.

He was suited up in two minutes, on his way to the truck that he'd seen next to the fire escape earlier, with its ladder extended all the way, reaching to the seventh floor. But some idiot stepped in his way as Cade tried to go around the corner. And he wouldn't move.

What the hell?

He recognized the features altered by a bad blond wig and a mustache at the same time that he spotted the gun. He barreled forward, movement in the full fire suit cumbersome and way too slow, wishing for a weapon once again.

David Smith squeezed off a shot, nicking the suit. Cade was on top of him the next second. But grabbing him wasn't easy in asbestos gloves. Damn Smith. So this was why none of his contacts had been able to find him in Indonesia recently.

Cade shoved his visor up with his shoulder. "What in hell are you doing here?" he shouted as they rolled.

"You would have come," Smith shouted back, looking like a man who thought he had the advantage.

"Damn right." Cade rolled them again, nearly losing his grip on Smith's gun hand. Damn the suit. He swore and slammed the front of his helmet into the man's face, heard the visor crack, then saw the blood bloom between Smith's eyes.

The bastard was right. Cade would have gone after him, even to the farthest reaches of hell. Smith had betrayed him that day. He was never going to forget that. He was never going to forget Pachi. He was never going to stop until Smith was dead.

But he'd been slowed down by the fact that he couldn't get any information on Smith until recently, when he'd finally contacted Abhi under a false identity and the guy had indicated that he had a lead for the right price. He could have contacted Abhi sooner. Could have gone to Indonesia himself to scare up some leads. But something had held him back. A glimpse of normal life perhaps. The anticipation of daily fights with Bailey, the sparks that flew and watching her sometimes through the window as she arranged and rearranged her crazy garden art in front of the house, cinnamon hair blowing in the breeze.

Bailey might already be dead.

The thought hit him harder than a live wire, snapping him back into the present. Smith took advantage of that split second and got on top, pinning Cade against the bars of a basement window.

He heard a window blow somewhere behind them. Smith did, too, and tried to move away from the cascade of glass. Now Cade held him in place, turning the tables. The flames roared behind the glass. But nothing happened.

"Luck is with me," Smith hissed between his teeth.

But the triumphant smile on his face didn't get a chance to settle in. The window behind him blew the next second, showering them with glass as flames shot out. Cade had protective gear on. Smith had nothing.

He shoved the man off as Smith struggled with his burning clothes. Given another second or two, Cade could have finished him off and had his revenge. Revenge had been his first thought when he'd woken after lung surgery. It had been the reason he had stayed alive. It had been the promise he'd made Pachi as the kid screamed, dying.

But now, instead of killing the bastard, Cade ran in the direction of the truck by the stairs.

Smith could make it. Burns or not, he had a fair chance. Someone could come around the corner and douse him, saving his sorry ass without ever knowing that he was saving a cold-blooded killer who was responsible for the murder of dozens. Smith was a wily bastard. If there was a way to escape this hell, he would find it. Then someday he would come back for Cade again.

But Cade didn't even look back to check on the man. Bailey was his only thought now, getting to her in time. He went around the back and saw the truck still in place. A fireman stood at the very top of the ladder, pouring water in a broken window with a hose.

Cade climbed up behind him.

The man was focused enough on what he was doing that he didn't notice anything until Cade already had a leg over on the fire escape.

The guy shouted after him, "It's ready to melt!"

Cade ignored the warning and swung his other leg

over, putting his full weight on the structure, which had gotten considerably less stable since he and Bailey had climbed it. Coming back this way was not an option. He spoke into the microphone inside his helmet. "Two jumpers up front. Start pumping the air bag." He climbed the rickety structure as fast as he could.

Damn, he was too old for this, he thought as he struggled over the edge. The suit weighed a ton. But he immediately forgot that when he couldn't spot Bailey. He rushed forward, searching. And there she was, rolled up in a ball, in the cover of a vent stack.

He crossed the roof in no time, pulling her up and putting the oxygen mask on her face. "They're waiting for us at the front." He picked her up when her knees buckled. Then they were on the edge at last, and he set her down to slip the mask off. He dropped it and shook off the tank, not wanting it to injure either of them.

The air bag waited below, insanely small and only partially inflated. Smoke and fire rolled at their backs. Fear flashed in her eyes as she held him in a death grip.

He pulled off the asbestos gloves so he could fully take her hand. "Take it easy. A few more minutes and we are out of here."

"If we make it… I was thinking while I waited, could you bring Pachaimani and his sister to the States? If you have to leave for work, I could keep an eye on them. Maybe Zak and Pachaimani could be friends. I think it might be good for both of them. Is that what you promised him? To get them out?"

Oh, man. He didn't want to go there, not now. He couldn't tell Bailey that he had promised Pachaimani to bring David Smith's black heart and lay it on the kid's grave. How he had shouted that to the boy as the kid had been trapped in the basement of the mansion with his sister, burning, while Cade was lying not ten feet from the barred door, choking on his own blood, his chest all torn up with shrapnel, and David Smith was up on that damned marble patio, just looking on and laughing.

The powers that be had considered the mission a great success. The money transfer had been stopped, and the terrorist group in question had been delivered a serious blow. Ruvaraj was dead.

He considered the day his worst failure, his worst nightmare—the one op he would never get over.

"Pachi is gone. They're dead." The smoke brought tears to his eyes, but he could still see Bailey's face go white under all the soot.

She leaned against him, nestling her face in the crook of his neck. Her tears felt wet against his skin. She was scared to death, in mortal danger, and crying for a couple of kids she'd never met, offering him comfort.

"Want to hear something insane?" He buried his nose in her smoky hair instead of looking down.

An air bag took ten minutes to inflate. Theirs had another five to go. Except that they couldn't hang out up here that long. He needed to calm Bailey for the jump, to get her thinking about something other than how dangerous their escape was going to be.

If the jump didn't go well, what was the one thing he would wish he had told her?

"It happened."

She looked up. "What?" Her voice shook.

"I fell in love." He dipped his head and brushed his sooty lips over hers. "I wish—"

She wouldn't let him finish. "I love you, too, Cade. Whatever happens." She squeezed his hand as they stepped off the ledge.

Epilogue

Cade sat by the lake, watching Bailey walk toward him on the sand, her cell phone stuck to her ear. He tucked Joey's wedding invitation back into the pile of mail next to him to share with her later. He never grew tired of watching her. She still took his breath away at every turn and he had a feeling it would stay that way to the end.

She came over, ready to slip into her beach chair next to his, but he reached out and grabbed her by the waist, bringing her down on top of him. He loved the way their bodies fit together. His was saluting hers already. It'd been at least two hours since they'd made love in the water.

She stifled a squeal as she said, "Bye, then," and hung up. She settled against him with a contented sigh, which warmed his heart like nothing ever had. "Zak wants to know if he can come down in a few weekends, when the house is finished."

"Are you crazy? I'm retired. My heart can't take looking after that kid. He needs a full commando unit to keep him out of trouble."

Which he was getting, sort of. Carly had taken to him, having been a misunderstood child genius herself. So she kept an eye on him remotely, and they kept in touch through the Internet. Carly was as bad as a full commando unit if she wanted to be. Badder.

Bailey lifted a sexy eyebrow. "You're only forty."

"Yeah, but think of the tough times I've been through, the neighbors I've had." He paused for effect. "Of course he can come."

"I guess, then, since you're retired and all that, you probably want to rest." She pulled away, but mischief twinkled in her beautiful blue-violet eyes.

"We can rest after." He pulled her right back, closer, and nibbled the soft skin of her neck.

"After what?" She played the innocent.

He made a rumbling sound in the back of his throat. "After we shake the shack."

She giggled.

Man, it was good to see her happy and carefree. He was going to make it his mission to keep her that way for as long as he lived. He'd kept her close through that hair-raising jump from the burning building and insisted on riding in the same ambulance with her and Zak to get checked out.

The Colonel had smoothed the way with the FBI. There had been an investigation, but it had been kept civilized. They had, however, put the fear of God in Zak. Which was fine with him. The kid needed to grow up to his skill level.

"It's hardly a shack." She glanced back at his house overlooking Lake Harmony, sitting on six acres of peaceful, private land, which was now fully secured with the best gadgets a man could get. He didn't take chances with the love of his life, no, sir. Not that any imminent danger threatened.

Smith had been caught at the burning building and been lumped in with the terrorists, who were part of a tribal group that played a large part in the African gun trade and stood to lose millions and considerable territory if peace was restored. Cade was the only person who knew the true reason why Smith had been there, and he wasn't about to tell the Feds. It wasn't a bad thing, Smith rotting in prison for the rest of his life. The bastard was facing charges of terrorism and was looking at life in a high-security prison as soon as he recovered from the burns on sixty-five percent of his body.

But Cade would have been lying if he said he wouldn't have liked to put the guy's lights out permanently. Personally. The urge still came from time to time, along with the knowledge that if he really wanted to, he could get to the bastard.

He would never forget Pachi.

But in the still of the night, with Bailey in his arms, his thoughts of revenge were more and more frequently supplanted by thoughts that he had to let go of the past. The best way to fight death was to live, and he planned on doing just that.

As a late surprise gift for his retirement, Nick and Joey had gone on an unofficially approved mission—meaning the Colonel had threatened them only with court-martial instead of a firing squad—

to Indonesia and had taken care of the last two men who still had a price on Cade's head. He no longer had to hide out at his uncle's place. A good thing since the contractor was dragging his feet getting started on it.

At least he'd been able to talk Bailey into staying with him here in the meanwhile. "So you like the house?"

"Love it."

"Enough to stay here with me forever? You can have the apartment on top of the garage for your workshop." They'd only been here for three months, and he already had a dozen wooden sunflowers dotting his otherwise pristine front lawn. And about a dozen garden flags. The woman couldn't help herself.

"Forever?" She drew back, growing serious.

"Forever."

A slow smile began to spread on her face. "What if I *didn't* like your house?"

"I have other houses." He kissed her with all the passion he felt for her. "Let's make beautiful garden art together for the rest of our lives."

That he should be so nervous waiting for her answer was damned disconcerting.

She seemed to be considering his idea. "I might move on to other hobbies eventually."

Thank God for that.

"Such as?" He kissed her throat. Nobody said he had to play fair.

"Tantric sex." She laughed, proving that she could hold her own in a dirty fight.

He shifted so she ended up under him. "You're killing me here."

"You make me believe in impossible things, like love." She smiled at him.

"You make me believe in impossible things, like leaving the past behind and becoming an ordinary man."

"You didn't hear that from me, that's for sure." She took his face between her hands. "Cade Palmer, you'll never be an ordinary man. But you're a good man. And I love you for that. Among other things," she added with a teasing smile after a moment.

"Will you marry me?" he asked, sliding his hands under her T-shirt, over her velvet skin, losing himself in the moment of anticipation, in the feel of her under his hands. He buried his face in her long, smooth neck. "I should warn you. I'll probably want kids."

"Boys like their daddy?" Her voice had gratifyingly weakened.

"Sweet little girls like their mom. And maybe one boy. Will you marry me?" he asked again, his mouth hovering over hers. "Have I mentioned that this is a very, very private beach?"

She wrapped her arms and legs around him and pressed those incredible lips of hers against his at last. "Yes."

* * * * *

Silhouette Desire kicks off 2009 with
MAN OF THE MONTH, *a yearlong*
program featuring incredible heroes
by stellar authors.

When Navy SEAL Hunter Cabot returns
home for some much-needed R & R,
he discovers he's a married man. There's
just one problem: he's never met his "bride."

Enjoy this sneak peek at Maureen Child's
AN OFFICER AND A MILLIONAIRE.
Available January 2009 from Silhouette Desire.

One

Hunter Cabot, Navy SEAL, had a healing bullet wound in his side, thirty days' leave and, apparently, a wife he'd never met.

On the drive into his hometown of Springville, California, he stopped for gas at Charlie Evans's service station. That's where the trouble started.

"Hunter! Man, it's good to see you! Margie didn't tell us you were coming home."

"Margie?" Hunter leaned back against the front fender of his black pickup truck and winced as his side gave a small twinge of pain. Silently then, he watched as the man he'd known since high school filled his tank.

Charlie grinned, shook his head and pumped gas. "Guess your wife was lookin' for a little 'alone' time with you, huh?"

"My—" Hunter couldn't even say the word. *Wife?* He didn't have a wife. "Look, Charlie…"

"Don't blame her, of course," his friend said with

a wink as he finished up and put the gas cap back on. "You being gone all the time with the SEALs must be hard on the ol' love life."

He'd never had any complaints, Hunter thought, frowning at the man still talking a mile a minute. "What're you—"

"Bet Margie's anxious to see you. She told us all about that R & R trip you two took to Bali." Charlie's dark brown eyebrows lifted and wiggled.

"Charlie…"

"Hey, it's okay, you don't have to say a thing, man."

What the hell could he say? Hunter shook his head, paid for his gas and as he left, told himself Charlie was just losing it. Maybe the guy had been smelling gas fumes too long.

But as it turned out, it wasn't just Charlie. Stopped at a red light on Main Street, Hunter glanced out his window to smile at Mrs. Harker, his second-grade teacher who was now at least a hundred years old. In the middle of the crosswalk, the old lady stopped and shouted, "Hunter Cabot, you've got yourself a wonderful wife. I hope you appreciate her."

Scowling now, he only nodded at the old woman—the only teacher who'd ever scared the crap out of him. What the hell was going on here? Was everyone but him nuts?

His temper beginning to boil, he put up with a few more comments about his "wife" on the drive through town before finally pulling into the wide, circular drive leading to the Cabot mansion. Hunter didn't have a clue what was going on, but he planned to get to the bottom of it. Fast.

He grabbed his duffel bag, stalked into the house and paid no attention to the housekeeper, who ran at him, fluttering both hands. "Mr. Hunter!"

"Sorry, Sophie," he called out over his shoulder as he took the stairs two at a time. "Need a shower, then we'll talk."

He marched down the long, carpeted hallway to the rooms that were always kept ready for him. In his suite, Hunter tossed the duffel down and stopped dead. The shower in his bathroom was running. His *wife?*

Anger and curiosity boiled in his gut, creating a churning mass that had him moving forward without even thinking about it. He opened the bathroom door to a wall of steam and the sound of a woman singing—off-key. Margie, no doubt.

Well, if she was his wife… Hunter walked across the room, yanked the shower door open and stared in at a curvy, naked, temptingly wet woman.

She whirled to face him, slapping her arms across her naked body while she gave a short, terrified scream.

Hunter smiled. "Hi, honey. I'm home."

* * * * *

Be sure to look for
AN OFFICER AND A MILLIONAIRE
by USA TODAY *bestselling author Maureen Child.*
Available January 2009 from Silhouette Desire.

CELEBRATE
60 YEARS
OF PURE READING PLEASURE
WITH **HARLEQUIN**®!

We'll be spotlighting a different series
every month throughout 2009
to celebrate our 60th anniversary.
Look for Silhouette Desire® in January!

MAN of the MONTH

Collect all 12 books in the Silhouette Desire®
Man of the Month continuity, starting in
January 2009 with *An Officer and a Millionaire*
by *USA TODAY* bestselling author
Maureen Child.

*Look for one new Man of the Month title
every month in 2009!*

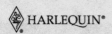

#1107 FAMILIAR VOWS by Caroline Burnes
Fear Familiar
Familiar's back! The crime-solving black cat detective was on the case of a killer targeting beautiful wedding photographer Michelle Sieck. But neither the killer nor Michelle knew they'd each have to go toe to toe with U.S. Marshal Lucas West.

#1108 SECRETS IN FOUR CORNERS by Debra Webb
Kenner County Crime Unit
Sheriff Patrick Martinez was the law in these parts of Colorado, and nobody was going to be intimidated under his watch—least of all his longtime love Bree Hunter and her little daughter, who he wished was his....

#1109 THE NIGHT IN QUESTION by Kelsey Roberts
The Rose Tattoo
For the life of her, Kresley Hayes could not explain how her unconscious body washed up on the shore in an evening gown. Lucky for her, FBI Agent Matthew DeMarco found her. Inexplicably reluctant to turn to the law for help, Kresley had to decide whether she could trust the handsome Matt with her life, let alone her heart.

#1110 BRANDED BY THE SHERIFF by Delores Fossen
Texas Paternity: Boots and Babies
When a family feud led to brutal murders in this Texas town, it was up to Sheriff Beck Tanner to protect single mother Faith Matthews and her baby from the killer. But Beck didn't expect to feel such fierce protectiveness over mother and child, especially when saving their lives meant facing off with his own family...

#1111 A VOICE IN THE DARK by Jenna Ryan
He's a Mystery
A serial killer's brutal attack left criminal profiler Noah Graydon scarred and determined to stay concealed from the world—that was, until he met Angel Carter, beautiful FBI agent and the killer's next target.

#1112 BETTER THAN BULLETPROOF by Kay Thomas
Ex-marine Harlan Jeffries thought he could handle anything...but when he found himself in the unlikely position of dodging bullets for Gina Rodgers and her orphaned nephew, he knew that more than his extreme protective instincts were motivating his actions.